Storm IN A TEACUP

A Tea & Sympathy Mystery

BOOK 7

J. NEW

Storm In A Teacup
A Tea & Sympathy Mystery
Book 7

Cover design: J. New.
Interior formatting: Alt 19 Creative

Other Books By J. New

The Yellow Cottage Vintage Mysteries in order:
The Yellow Cottage Mystery (Free)
An Accidental Murder
The Curse of Arundel Hall
A Clerical Error
The Riviera Affair
A Double Life

The Finch & Fischer Mysteries in order:
Decked in the Hall
Death at the Duck Pond
Battered to Death

Tea & Sympathy Mysteries in order:
Tea & Sympathy
A Deadly Solution
Tiffin & Tragedy
A Bitter Bouquet
A Frosty Combination
Steeped in Murder

Chapter One

LILLY TWEED PULLED back her hair and struggled to clip it up.

"I really must do something with my hair," she said, wincing as she pulled and tried to force an errant curl into the band.

"Are you talking about colouring the grey?" Stacey, her shop manager, asked in all innocence.

Lilly looked at her and burst out laughing.

"Well, I am now! I actually meant just getting it cut."

"Oops. Sorry."

"Don't worry, you're right. There seems to be a lot more grey than brown nowadays. I'm wondering if I should just let it go and grow old gracefully?"

"Grey hair is really cool now," Stacey said. "Loads of celebrities and actresses are doing it. I think it looks great."

"Really? Might be worth thinking about. I honestly can't be faffed with going to the hairdresser every month to sit for hours while it's coloured."

She opened the foot stool and set it in front of the tall stockroom shelves. Her order of spring tea sets had arrived a few weeks ago, and she'd been gradually moving them from the storeroom to the main shop ever since.

One of her favourites, a lovely vintage cabbage rose design, she'd almost forgotten about until Stacey had queried what had happened to the order. Now, they were over halfway through spring and only just adding them to the displays.

"Finding these sets now is good timing when you think about it," Stacey said from where she stood on the floor below Lilly, ready to take the boxes from her. "We've completely sold out of the sunflower sets, so bringing out the rose ones will give me an opportunity to do some on-line promotional stuff. I'll get them dusted and put on display today, then take some pictures. At the very least, it should remind the locals to come in and restock their tea. Maybe we could even run a sale on one of the rose teas we've got a surplus of to add to the excitement?"

"That's a great idea. I'll look over the inventory tonight and let you know what we can do a promotion on," Lilly said, carefully passing down the boxes of fragile china to the waiting girl, who placed them on a nearby table.

It had been almost a year ago to the day that Lilly had first employed the young American. She'd appeared in the shop in answer to the help wanted sign in the window and immediately started to assist the cleanup of a breakage as though she'd already got the job. She'd known nothing about teas and Lilly had been dubious to start with, but Stacey had been genuinely interested in her desire to learn more.

She'd arrived in Plumpton Mallet to attend the local university while also getting to know her estranged father, a London native, who was a four-hour train journey away. Up until that time, she'd known very little about her English Heritage. Stacey had officially started work at Lilly's Tea Emporium the day after she'd first turned up, and was now not only the manager of the tea shop but The Agony Aunt's cafe which Lilly owned with a friend.

Employing Stacey had turned out to be one of the best decisions Lilly had made for her businesses. She'd taken to the study of teas like the proverbial duck to water. She'd brought Lilly's shop on-line with an all singing all dancing website, and produced some excellent graphic designs and marketing material. She was also friendly, knowledgeable and highly personable with everyone who came through the door, and as a result, was extremely popular with all the customers. Locals and tourists alike.

Stacey's designs for the take away mugs over the Christmas season had been exceptionally good, so much so that people were asking when the next design would be available, as they wanted to collect them all. Lilly made a mental note to ask Stacey to design a spring version, with a view to having the four seasons each year made as collectibles.

"Right, that's the last box," Lilly said, getting down from the ladder. The two of them then began transferring everything to the main shop.

Earl Grey, the former stray now official shop cat, was asleep in his usual spot in the window, his damaged ear twitching at the sound of them entering. But that was the sum total of his movement. He didn't even open an eye when a small boy walking through the market square with his mother tapped on the glass to get his attention.

Stacey had asked for an antique oak table to be put in the centre of the shop floor to set out the new spring display, and while she began, Lilly went to top up the cat's water and food bowls. That done, she gave him a final scratch behind his ears, which elicited the loudest of purrs although his eyes remained closed, and went to check the post basket.

Prior to opening the shop, Lilly had worked for The Plumpton Mallet Gazette, the local newspaper, as their Agony Aunt. She had been made redundant when a larger concern bought the paper, but the payout she'd been given had let her fund the opening of her Tea Emporium. However, the locals had apparently missed her good advice and had started posting letters at the shop. Eventually, she had fitted a designated letterbox which dropped the mail into a basket inside.

"Any letters today?" Stacey asked, smoothing out a snowy white damask tablecloth and checking the levels on either side were the same.

"Just one," Lilly replied, locking the basket and moving behind the counter to the till and wrapping area.

It was her favourite part in the shop. Plumpton Mallet was one of the oldest towns in the north of the country, steeped in a rich history, and as such many of the shops had started out life as something different from what they were trading as today. The Tea Emporium had once been the town's only apothecary shop, and all subsequent owners had kept as many fixtures and fittings from the original design as possible. Lilly had done the same, and designed the entire vintage scheme around the floor to ceiling cabinet on the wall behind the counter, with shelves in the upper half and dozens of small drawers with brass handles in the lower. The drawers contained all the tea samples, with the shelves used for displaying sale items. The top of the base unit housed different kettles in various designs to boil the water for brewing customer samples. Along the bar-style counter were several tall wooden stools where customers would sit and drink the teas before choosing the ones they wished to purchase.

Lilly sat at the bar near the antique till, taking her time to read the letter. She smiled. It was asking her for her favourite spring dessert recipes. Much more light hearted than some of the letters she received. She absentmindedly chewed the end of her pen while thinking of a suitable response. She chose two: white tea infused chocolate pots with pistachio toffee, and meringue roulade with orange and passion fruit. Luckily, she kept the full recipes on her phone.

She'd just finished her reply when the shop phone rang.

"THE TEA EMPORIUM," she answered.

"It's Abigail," the voice at the other end boomed.

Lilly grinned. "I'm surprised to get a call from you during the lunch rush. Are you busy over there?"

"Always. It's compete madness and we're running out of the new tea blend... the lemon and lavender."

"Don't worry," Lilly assured her. "I'll bring a couple of boxes down."

"You're a lifesaver. Thank you," Abigail said, hanging up the phone without so much as a proper goodbye. Abigail could be a tad dramatic at times, but Lilly knew if she said she was running out of tea, then it was imminent. The lemon lavender had proved to be immensely popular. It was her own creation, only her second, the first being a peppermint and cranberry she'd made especially for Christmas. That had also sold well.

"Was that the cafe?" Stacey asked. "Is it urgent?"

"They're running out of the new blend. I need to rush some over there."

"Wow, people have been going through that really quickly. You're going to have to make some more tonight because we'll run out here, too, if you take some down to Abigail. Probably by the end of the day."

"Really? Well, that's my evening sorted out then. What an exciting life I lead," Lilly laughed, grabbing a couple of boxes and waving to Stacey as she left the shop for the quick walk down to the cafe.

The Agony Aunt's cafe was her most recent investment. After the former owner put the property up for sale at a low price due to serious personal issues, Lilly and Abigail, another former agony aunt at the paper and Lilly's old nemesis, had gone into business together. The cafe had grown substantially since they'd taken over and completely refurbished the interior. They'd even added a special art déco style tearoom at the back for people to hire for special occasions.

Abigail came running to meet her at the front door and, much to Lilly's delight, already had two take away lunch bags prepared for her and Stacey.

"It looks as though you're on top of things," Lilly said. "How did you know I would order lunch? And how did you know what I'd want?"

"It's a thank you for bringing the tea. And you and Stacey almost always order the same thing," Abigail replied, taking the tea from Lilly's outstretched hand. "Anyway, must dash. I'll call you when things slow down. Don't forget we have a meeting here after we close today."

"Don't worry, I'll be here," Lilly replied, and taking her lunch, returned to her shop.

THE TEA EMPORIUM'S usual rush time was just after lunch, so she and Stacey had time to eat in peace before the crowds arrived. She was quite surprised to find the young girl had almost finished the new spring display and had added a large vase of realistic silk cabbage roses, their best napkins and silver napkin rings, along with other small additions like the battery operated tea-lights they'd just started to stock, to the display of rose and other spring design tea sets. It looked absolutely stunning.

"Stacey, this looks absolutely incredible. It wouldn't look out of place in Country Homes and Garden magazine."

"That's the plan," Stacey said, snapping several pictures for their website and social media pages. "I should have a number of them up on-line by this afternoon and I'll send a newsletter out to our customers. Then all we have to do is wait for the rush. Ooo what's in the bags?"

"Our favourite lunch each, courtesy of Abigail. We may as well eat out here as the shop is empty. Besides, I want to take time to admire your display. I've got a meeting after we close over at the cafe. Abigail and I need to discuss the final details for the 16th birthday party we're catering. I'm quite excited about it. The parents of the birthday boy are coming over, so we're getting together just before to make sure our presentation is up to scratch."

"Sounds like fun," Stacey said, grabbing her lunch. "So I'm manning the shop and overseeing the cafe that day?"

"If that's all right with you? Basically, it will be up to you to put out any fires while Abigail and me are away, although with Fred in charge at the cafe I doubt there'll be anything too serious."

"It's at the rowing club, the party, is that right?"

"Yes, which is at the reservoir out on the north road. About half an hour from here."

"I've never been rowing. Seems a bit lax of me considering I'm majoring in sports therapy. I'd like to give it a try sometime."

"I'll go with you, if you like? I used to row for my school, although only on the second team. I wasn't quite good enough for the first. But it is great fun. Unless you're in a boat with Archie, that is, then you tend to get drenched."

Lilly was referring to the trip she and Archie had taken a couple of weeks prior. At the hotel where they'd stopped for lunch, there was a large lake with rowing boats for hire. Archie had insisted on being the gentleman and taken the oars. Lilly laughed when she thought about it now. For the first ten minutes, they'd gone round in circles while Archie got used to being back in a boat after many years. After that, it went downhill and they'd both ended up soaking wet.

"You'd take me rowing?" Stacey asked, bringing Lilly back to the present.

"Absolutely. It's been a long time since I've been. We could go at the weekend if you want?"

"I'd love to."

"The rowing club would be the best place to go. Plus, I'll be able to have a walk around and familiarise myself with the place before we set up the event this weekend."

"Great! Is Sunday okay?" Stacey asked, eyes gleaming with excitement.

"Perfect. Right, we better get on. Lunch is over and the shoppers are going to be flooding the market square any minute."

Chapter Two

AS THE DAY drew to a close, Lilly left Stacey locking up and set off back to the cafe for the meeting. The weather was still beautiful; the sun shining between whisks of white clouds, although there was a slight chill in the air now as the evening began to fall.

"Hi, Lilly," a fellow shop owner called out, as she turned the door sign from open to closed.

"Hello, Sue. How's business with you these days?"

"It's picking up a bit, thankfully. You know how it is. An ice-cream shop doesn't ever do a roaring trade during the winter months. Actually, I've been thinking about expanding my offerings a bit during the colder months. Maybe hot cocoa and pasties. What do you think? You're great at that sort of thing. Do you have any suggestions?"

"I think both of those are great ideas," Lilly said. "I'd be happy to drop in one day and have a chat about it. With winter over now, you have months to plan and advertise something new."

"That would be great, Lilly. Thank you."

"How about we sit down for tea one evening this week? I'll have a think about some concepts in the meantime."

"Perfect," Sue said. "I look forward to it."

The cafe closed half an hour later than the tea shop, so there were still a handful of customers just finishing their meals inside when Lilly entered. The head barista was Frederick Warren, Stacey's boyfriend and fellow student. He waved a greeting and gave her a huge grin.

"The Stapletons should be here soon," Abigail said to Lilly, turning the door sign to closed. "I have the menu samples printing now. Fred, would you bring them through when they've finished?"

"Will do," he said, beginning to close the station as the last of the customers paid their bill.

Lilly and Abigail made their way through to the tearoom, which they'd decorated for spring. Along with small and large vases of seasonal silk flowers, they'd also decided to rotate the wall art according to the season, but still in-keeping with the overall art déco design. Lilly's favourite was entitled Spring by Alphonse Mucha, closely followed by Gustav Klimt's Flower Garden.

At the central table where they would speak with the clients, Abigail had placed several spring tea sets. They would be serving various tea samples for them to choose from, which went with the set menus they'd devised for the party. Abigail had also lit a few lemon and mandarin tea lights and placed them in cut glass art déco style holders, which added to the ambiance and gave a sense of peace and happiness.

"You're really on top of things," Lilly said, admiring the display. "It's gorgeous in here."

"Well, other than the Christmas Market, this is the first event I've done with you. And it's the cafe's very first catering event, so I really want it to go well."

"There's no need to impress me, Abigail. The cafe couldn't be in better hands. You've achieved a huge amount since you've been running it and it's improving day by day. I'm absolutely certain the clients will be just as impressed as I am."

"I really appreciate that, Lilly. I so want this cafe to work out. Especially after my career as an agony aunt was such a disaster," Abigail said with a sad smile and a heavy sigh as she laid out the various menu samples Fred had just brought through.

"Actually," Lilly said, handing one of the printed sheets back to her partner. "I think we should scrap this one. This tea blend didn't sell at all well and as the menu is based around it, I don't think it will work."

"Really? That's such a shame. I quite liked that tea."

"Yes, I did too. But it is obviously an acquired taste, and if the public doesn't like it, then there's no point using it. I'm a fan of unusual teas, but we're catering for a 16-year-old boy's birthday party, so it's not a great option. But last night I came up with several non-alcoholic cocktails, which I'm sure will work better."

"That's a great idea. Do you have samples?"

"I do. They are in your fridge. I'll get them after they've sampled everything else. Sorry for the late notice." Abigail waved the comment away. "I've named them after famous rowers. So we have the Redgrave Raspberry Refresher, the Pinsent Pink Punch, Whipple Watermelon Spritzer, Morin's Minty Tea Punch and Searle's Celebration Punch. There are also several smoothies on the menu, which are simple to make."

"Genius!" Abigail said. "I never would have thought of it. But every sixteen-year-old wants to feel like a grown up, even if what they're drinking has no alcohol in it. And what's even better is they are all healthy, and considering we're serving sports people, that's a great selling point. Susanna Stapleton is a very keen tennis player you know, and runs marathons, so I'm sure she'll appreciate the effort. Well done, Lilly. Hang on, I'd better get cocktail glasses, ice and some of those little umbrellas. Let me just go and ask Fred to find what he can and bring it all through. Gosh, I do love it when everything comes together like this."

A few minutes later, she was back with the tea samples in a carved wooden box, and with Fred in tow carrying cocktail paraphernalia.

"This looks great," he said. "Makes me wish I was sixteen again."

"Really?" Lilly asked.

Fred shook his head, grinning. "No, not really. I'm having more fun now than I ever did when I was sixteen. Give me a shout if you need me for anything else."

"Will do, thanks, Fred," Abigail said.

"Oh, by the way, I've just seen the Stapletons walking across the square. They'll be here any minute. Shall I show them through?"

"Yes, please."

SUSANNA STAPLETON WAS the one who had hired them to cater for the party, so both Lilly and Abigail had met her before. She approached with a smile and held out her hand. "Thank you for meeting us today. I'm looking forward to seeing what you've come up with. This is my husband Edgar. He's a big fan of the cafe."

"Very nice to meet you both," Edgar Stapleton said, also shaking their hands. "My wife is right. I come here every Thursday for lunch. It's become a weekly custom that I look forward to."

"I thought I recognised you," Abigail said. "I believe I served you last week myself?"

"I believe you did."

Lilly indicated the chairs and invited the couple to sit.

"These are the preliminary menus we've worked on. If you want to look them over and let us know if there are any changes you'd like. They have been designed to compliment both the teas and the range of non-alcoholic cocktails we've put together especially for the occasion. And of course, we're going to provide you with samples of everything now. How about we start with the lemon and lavender tea?" Lilly suggested, and with nods of confirmation from the Stapletons, Abigail got to work.

As Lilly had hoped, once they had tried all the samples, they chose the menu based on the lemon lavender blend. They also were thrilled with the idea of all the cocktails and thanked Lilly profusely for going to such an effort.

"Is Peter looking forward to the party?" Lilly asked.

"He really is," Susanna said. "Oh, that reminds me, we've an updated list. A few more attendees. I hope that's all right?" Lilly said, of course it was. Susanna reached into her handbag and withdrew a sheet of paper.

"You've crossed out Victoria's name?" Edgar said, looking at the list over his wife's shoulder. "Why can't she come?"

Susanna gave an exasperated sigh. "Edgar, Peter and Victoria have broken up." It was clear from her tone she thought her husband should know this information.

"Did they? That's a shame. I quite liked that girl. So, what happened?"

"I've honestly no idea, Edgar. You know what teenagers are like. But I agree with you, it is a shame they made a lovely couple."

"I wonder why he didn't tell me?" Edgar mused.

"He doesn't like talking about this sort of thing, you know that. Especially to his parents. It's a teenage thing. I expect he'll share when he's ready."

Lilly and Abigail had been sitting quietly, listening to the couples' conversation. As soon as there was a lull, Abigail spoke.

"So, is this the complete guest list?"

"Yes, that's everybody," Susanna said. "I thought it would be a nice idea to add personalised name cards at the tables if it's not too windy. Would that be acceptable?"

"Yes, of course," Lilly said. "I can devise something that will hang from the cups or the glasses. That way, if it is a little breezy, they won't blow away. I've found they make quite nice little gifts for the guests to remember the occasion."

"Oh, what a very good idea," Susanna said. "Perhaps something in-keeping with the rowing theme? Do you have anything like that?"

Lilly was about to say no but she could do some research when Abigail interrupted her.

"Do you know, I think I may have just the thing. One moment."

She left briefly and returned with a couple of nautical themed luggage tags in blue, red and white. One side where the name of the guest could be written, the other with designs of a yacht or a ship's wheel. The tag tie could be then be threaded through a cup handle, or wrapped round a napkin.

"What about these? They're hand painted wood, light, but very robust. A friend of mine makes them."

"Oh, these would be perfect," Susanna said. "What do you think?" she said, turning to her husband.

"Yes. I like them. Nice idea. Oh, and while I remember, you'd better add Preston to the list," he added, receiving a sharp glance from his wife. "He called today to say he's coming home to see Peter and celebrate his birthday. It's been a while since the boys have been together."

"Your son is coming?" Susanna said in a displeased voice.

Lilly could feel the sudden tension in the room. Susanna looked annoyed, and Edgar looked irritated at his wife's tone.

"Yes, your stepson is coming," he said now, obviously trying not to sound peeved in front of their hosts but failing miserably.

Susanna cleared her throat, catching her husband's mood and realised she needed to buck up a bit. "Wonderful news. What day is he coming? I'll make a big family dinner."

"Tomorrow."

"Oh, so he's coming for the week?"

"That's right. It will be good to spend some time with him."

"Won't it?" Susanna said with a smile that didn't reach her eyes. "It will be nice for him to have a week with home cooked food. It will make a change from the college food he's used to."

"Thank you," Edgar said, with a smile as tight as his wife's. He turned to Abigail and Lilly, looking flushed and uncomfortable. "Is that all you need?"

"I believe so," Lilly said, adding Preston Stapleton's name to the list. "We'll have the place names made and will be in touch about the seating arrangements soon."

"Actually," Susanna said, as she and her husband stood. "I thought I might come and help you set up. I'll be there early to put up the decorations, anyway. This way, it will save you the job."

"Of course, that's fine," Lilly said. "In that case, I believe all the decisions have been made. If there's anything last minute I need to ask you about, I'll give you a call."

"Thank you both," Susanna said, and with final goodbyes, she and her husband left the premises.

Lilly and Abigail breathed a sigh of relief.

"PHEW!" LILLY SAID, raising her eyebrows at Abigail. "That got a bit uncomfortable. I wonder what it was all about?"

"It's the connection between the Stapleton's and Lord and Lady Defoe, I expect."

The Defoe family was Plumpton Mallet's version of royalty, Lords and Ladies going back several generations.

"What connection is that?" Lilly asked.

"Lady Defoe's sister was Preston Stapleton's mother."

"Was?"

Abigail nodded. "Yes. She died. I only heard about it at the book club. You know what a hotbed of gossip it is. The books, as far as I can tell, are just an excuse to get together and dish the dirt. Apparently, she was still a teenager when she met Edgar Stapleton. Unfortunately, she became pregnant. You can imagine the scandal that ensued. They weren't married, obviously. Rumour has it she gave birth to Preston and as soon as they could Lady Defoe's parents gave the child to Edgar, told him to keep quiet and washed their hands of the whole affair. I assume he was given some hush money. Of course, secrets like that get out, eventually."

"Gosh, if that's true, it's awful," Lilly said, wondering if some of the information had been embellished at the source to add to the drama.

Abigail nodded. "As soon as he was able, Edgar shipped Preston off to boarding school, so there aren't many around here now who even know about it."

"Well, now I'm aware of their history, it seems to me that Susanna would prefer to keep it that way. Poor boy. How old is he, do you know?"

"I'm not sure, but he's studying at university so late teens, early twenties, I assume. Mind you, if he's making the effort to come to his brother's birthday party, then they must have a reasonably good relationship? Nothing like the gossips at the book club suggested."

"If it was discussed at Mrs Davenport's book club, then I'd take it all with a pinch of salt," Lilly said. "I'm surprised to hear it's still going after what happened last summer."

"I was surprised as well, actually," Abigail said, then blushed furiously. "Do you remember how I treated you that day?"

Lilly laughed. "It's hard to forget. But it's what you did after that really takes the biscuit."

"Oh, Lilly, I was so dreadful. I am sorry."

"Don't be silly, Abigail. You were going through an awful lot at the time. It's water under the bridge. And look how far we've come in the year since."

"Enemies, to friends and business partners. Who would have thought it?"

Chapter Three

IT WAS SUNDAY, the tea shop was closed, and as per their previous discussion, Lilly drove Stacey up to the reservoir to visit the location for the event, and to hire one of the boats so she could take Stacey out rowing for the first time.

"Wow, I can't believe I haven't been here before," Stacey said, as they meandered up the path alongside the lake on their way to the boathouse. Passing joggers and dog walkers as they went. "It's really beautiful. How big is it?"

Lilly laughed. "Somehow I knew you would ask me that, so I looked it up before we came out."

"Now why didn't I think to do that? Go on then, give me your best tour guide spiel."

Lilly cleared her throat. "Ladies and gentlemen, if you look to your right, you will see the reservoir. The surface area is 63 hectares, and the capacity is approximately 633 million gallons." Stacey stared at her with eyes wide and mouth open. "I know. Amazing isn't it?" Lilly said. "It provides the water for Plumpton Mallet and the surrounding villages. There are also several more reservoirs supplying water to the other immediate areas. The water is held in place by a small dam on the East side, which eventually flows into the river. The rowing club has another boathouse on the river itself for professional practice. There's been quite a few of our teams rowed at the Olympics, as well as national and international regattas and head races."

"Really? I thought it was more like messing about on the water. I didn't realise they trained proper sports people."

"This reservoir is for both. Training those who are new to the sport with the intentions of hopefully making some sort of career from it, and recreational for those who just want a day out. That's why all the boats are different," Lilly said, pointing to the various types of craft either moored up or already out on the water. "We'll take one of the bigger boats with fixed seats. Another thing I think you'll find interesting, beneath the water, is the remains of New Hall, once owned by a very prominent local family. Construction started in 1871, so I assume it was sold off around that time."

"They flooded a family home?"

"They did. It was a huge country estate which included all the surrounding land for as far as your eye can see," Lilly said, waving expansively to reinforce her point. "I expect the family was well compensated, though."

"Who owns it all now?" Stacey asked, as they approached the vast two storey boathouse. The rear half of the ground floor nearest the lake was used for storage of the boats, life-jackets, oars and other paraphernalia associated with rowing, the front half contained the reception area, an office and a small bar with display cases showing off the club's history. While the upper part consisted of a much larger bar and club room with various seating areas. It was a combination of a local pub and a private club. To the side was a large patio area, which was where the birthday party would be held.

"The land and lake are owned by the water authority, but the rowing club owns the building and pays a nominal rent for the land it sits on to the water board. The club is actually a charity, so makes its money from membership fees, fundraisers and sponsorships. And the hiring out for private events, such as the one we're doing."

"Cool," Stacey said. "Hey, Lilly, look over there. Talking of the event, I think that's the birthday boy." She pointed to a group of youths at the water's edge. "He tagged the teashop on-line in a post about his birthday next weekend. I recognise his face."

"Well spotted, Stacey. Let's go and say hello."

"Hello, Peter Stapleton?" Lilly asked as they approached the end of the path at the top of the bank.

Peter glanced up, a tall, blond, fresh-faced young man with a rowers physique. He was eating an apple. "Yes?"

"Hi, I'm Lilly Tweed and this is Stacey Pepper. My partner Abigail and I are doing the catering for your birthday party at the weekend."

"Oh, hi," he said, standing and jogging up the shallow wooden steps to meet her and Stacey, followed by his two friends. He stuck out his hand. "Nice to meet you both. And thanks for doing the party."

"You're very welcome."

Peter gestured to the two young men behind him. "These are my friends Oscar and Quintin. We're on the rowing team together," he explained.

"You're practicing today?"

"We hope so," Peter replied.

Stacey glanced at the boat they had been congregating round earlier. "You're two team members short?"

Peter grimaced. "Looks like it."

"We've lost two team members," Oscar told them.

"Hang on, Oscar," Peter said. "We've only lost one. Alison has only missed a couple of practices. And she sent me a text to say she had something else to do today."

"She could have texted you sooner. We've dragged the boat down already and practicing with one missing is bad enough, but with two?" he shrugged. "We might have to change disciplines."

Peter shook his head. "No need for that, Oscar. Alison is still part of the team. It won't be too hard to find one more."

"If she's still in the team, then she should be here," Oscar said, not prepared to let it lie.

Quintin punched Oscar lightly on the arm. "Give her a break, Oscar. She's off doing something for Pete's party."

"Oh. Well, how was I supposed to know?"

Peter laughed. "So much for that secret. Maybe we should call it a day?"

To Lilly's surprise, Stacey cleared her throat. "Actually, I'm a complete beginner. In fact, I've never even been in a rowing boat. And Lilly is a bit out of practice, but we can make up the numbers if you want? What do you think, Lilly?"

Lilly looked at the sportswear the kids were wearing, then down at her own boots, jeans and lightweight fleece. Stacey was similarly attired, although she had on trainers. "We're not exactly dressed for it."

"It'll get a bit cold out on the water, right?" Stacey said. "We should be okay."

Lilly could see Stacey really wanted to get out on the water with the team, so she smiled and nodded. "It's okay with me, if the boys don't mind."

"Are you sure?" Peter asked.

"Of course. It won't be the same as practicing with your full team, but it's better than not going out at all, isn't it? Besides, it will be fun."

Peter turned to his friends and asked what they thought.

"Yes, okay," Quintin said with a goofy smile.

Oscar shrugged. "Better than coming all this way for nothing, I suppose."

Peter gave Stacey a run through of the basics, what to do with two oars and what to expect from a sliding seat. She nodded, listening intently. "Okay, I think I've got it. I'll shout if I'm having problems."

Soon they were in the water and slowly gliding away from the bank. It the middle of the lake they began to pick up speed, with Peter continually shouting instructions.

"This is really cool," Stacey yelled, in order to be heard above the wind whipping past their ears.

"Hey, slow down!" Oscar snapped from where he sat behind her. "You've got to keep in rhythm with the rest of us. It's supposed to be a team event, not one person showing off. Honestly, I don't think girls and rowing is a good mix, Pete!"

"Wow," Stacey said. "I bet you're popular with girls," which caused the other two boys to laugh. Stacey didn't see, but Lilly gave a slight grimace from her position at the rear of the boat. This was the son of her latest clients and his friends. She didn't want reports of either her or her staff being rude to get back to Peter's parents. But it appeared the other boys were on Stacey's side.

"Just ignore him," Quintin said. "He's just trying to rile you up."

"Oscar," Peter said. "Calm down, mate. They're doing us a big favour here. The least you can be is polite."

"I was just messing around," Oscar said. The two boys ignored him.

After that, the rest of the trip to the far end of the lake and back went without a hitch, and both Lilly and Stacey enjoyed themselves immensely.

They said goodbye to the boys, who insisted there was no need to help return to the boat to the store, and walked along the track back to the car.

"That was great fun," Stacey said. "And I got a great workout. Although my arms are a bit sore. Thanks for inviting me, Lilly."

"You're welcome. I'm glad you enjoyed it. It was nice to be able to get to know Peter a little before the event. They were nice kids."

Stacey nodded. "They were. Although Oscar is a bit sulky. Must be teenage hormones or something."

Lilly laughed. Stacey was only six years older than them, yet she sounded like their mother.

"Come on, I'll take the scenic route back and you can see the rest of the countryside. It's really beautiful up here, especially in the spring."

Chapter Four

LILLY HURRIED THROUGH the cafe, arms laden with the last of the items needed for the birthday party. It was the morning of the event, and after making sure Stacey had everything she needed at the tea shop, she had driven round to the back of the cafe to help Abigail load everything into the boot of her car.

Abigail was currently going through a last-minute check with Fred, who was to be in charge during their absence. With the two of them being away for the rest of the day, they knew both the tea shop and the cafe were being left in capable hands.

"All set?" Lilly asked Abigail as she got in the passenger's seat.

"I think so. I must say I'm looking forward to it. I have a feeling it's all going to go very well. And look at the weather. We couldn't have asked for a more perfect day, could we? Oh, you did pack the cocktail recipes, didn't you? I won't be able to remember it all if it isn't written down."

"Don't worry, I've brought them," Lilly said, with a smile at her friend. "I went over the list at least four times. I'm sure we've got everything we need."

"I'm glad I managed to get the little umbrellas in the three club colours. I think they'll look fabulous."

"And who knew there were such things as blue maraschino cherries? I hope they don't stain everyone's mouth and lips blue."

"Lilly! I never thought of that! Oh, that would be awful. I don't think we should use them."

Lilly tried, but couldn't control her giggling.

"Oh Abigail, you are priceless. I'm sure they've been tested. They'll be fine. I was joking."

"Oh, for heaven's sake. I'm nervous enough without you making jokes," Abigail said, but she was smiling.

As they left Plumpton Mallet behind, travelling along the country road to the reservoir, Lilly mentioned she'd taken Stacey rowing the previous weekend. "We met Peter Stapleton up there, actually, with a couple of his rowing team friends."

"Oh? Did you stay to watch them practice?"

Lilly laughed. "You won't believe this, Abigail, but Stacey and me practiced with them. A couple of their teammates hadn't shown up, so we took their places."

"Really? That was brave of you. How did Stacey do?"

"Considering it was her first time, very well. Peter showed her the ropes and gave us both tips and tricks as we went. It was good fun."

"I think my arms would have fallen off if I'd had to row that far."

"To be honest, I was quite sore the next day. Stacey was fine, though."

"Well, she's much younger and fitter than we are, Lilly."

"Very true. But I'm extremely glad I've got some natural extra padding on my bum."

There were two parking areas at the reservoir. The one where Lilly had parked when she had taken Stacey was little more than a clearing in a wooded area just off the main road. She'd parked there deliberately, wanting to walk alongside the lake to show Stacey the area better. This time, however, with a boot full of catering supplies, Lilly parked in the designated car-park at the boat house.

The sound of the engine had caught the attention of Susanna Stapleton, who was busy laying tablecloths on the picnic benches with the help of a teen girl. Lilly waved as she and Abigail got out of the car, and the two of them hurried over to help with the unloading.

"Hello there," Susanna said. "You've arrived in perfect time. We've just finished laying the cloths so we're all ready for you. This is Alison, by the way," she added, introducing the girl with her. "One of Peter's friends."

"Nice to meet you both," Alison said.

"You too," Lilly said. "You're on the rowing team, aren't you? Peter mentioned you last weekend when Stacey and me were here."

"That's right," the girl said proudly. "Although they better get their acts together if they still want me on the team in time for the next competition."

"Oh, dear," Abigail said, opening the boot of the car and retrieving the first of the boxes. "That sounds a bit serious. What have they done?"

Alison shrugged. "Oh, you know, stupid male drama."

Susanna laughed. "That's right, you keep them on their toes, Alison. Now, we're here to help, so just show us where you would prefer everything," she said to Lilly and Abigail.

"Oh, here's Preston," Alison said, glancing at the far end of the car-park.

Lilly saw the immediate tension in Susanna's shoulders and followed Alison's gaze. He was a tall, slim young man dressed in black ripped jeans, a loose black shirt, and biker boots. His dark hair was combed back and hung to his shoulders. Lilly could see the sun glinting off the silver piercings in both ears and his left eyebrow.

Susanna exhaled. "That's my stepson. I apologise for his appearance. I'd hoped he would be a little more presentable."

"Don't worry, he said he'd change for the party if you wanted," Alison said.

"Actually, I was referring to those grotesque piercings," Susanna replied with a disappointed and haughty shake of her head. "He's been helping Peter decorate his room this week as well. I wouldn't be surprised if he's still got paint underneath his nails."

Alison shared a look with Lilly and rolled her eyes. First, making sure that Susanna didn't see her.

ALISON GAVE A brief wave to Peter's half-brother, then grabbing a box, followed Abigail and Susanna down to the seating area. Lilly was lifting the box of cocktail supplies when Preston appeared by her side and introduced himself.

"Can I help you with that?"

"Yes, please. It's one of the heavier ones. Full of breakables."

He grinned. "Don't worry, I'll be careful. I'm stronger than I look." Lilly smiled and assumed that was more wishful thinking than actually the case. They walked side by side to the awaiting tables. "I think my brother is excited about the party."

"That's good to know."

"Dad's been waxing lyrical about the food and tea at your cafe ever since I got home. I'll try to visit while I'm in town."

"You'll be very welcome, Preston."

"Hey Alison," he called out, putting the box on the nearest table. "How's the team doing this year?"

"Quite well, actually. We're in with a real chance of a medal or two if it all goes according to plan."

"Good news. Keeping my little brother in check, I hope?"

Alison laughed. "Of course. Someone has to!"

"So, Susanna, sorry I didn't get here earlier. What can I do to help?" Preston asked his stepmother.

"I think we'll be fine without your assistance, Preston," Susanna replied, without looking round.

Alison frowned. "But you were just saying how much there was to do and worried we wouldn't finish in time. Maybe he could blow up the balloons?"

Lilly noticed Susanna looked displeased for a second, before plastering on a smile. "You know, that's a good idea, Alison," she said, throwing a large bag of dark blue, light blue, and white balloons, the rowing team colours, in Preston's direction. He caught it in one hand and went to sit at one of the tables, tearing open the bag.

While Susanna took Alison to help hang the bunting, Abigail and Lilly started on the outside bar area.

After half an hour of blowing up balloons, Lilly noticed the boy was looking distinctly light-headed so brewed him a cup of tea and took it over.

"You really should take breaks when blowing up this many balloons, you know? You'll be keeling over in a dead faint if you're not careful."

"I wasn't expecting to do it this way. I'm surprised Susanna didn't bring a manual pump. She usually remembers everything. That tea smells amazing. Lemon and Lavender?" Lilly nodded. "Thanks very much. I was getting pretty thirsty. So, what can I help you with now?"

Lilly smiled. Preston, for all his outward appearance screaming semi Gothic punk, was quite a gentleman. He helped set up the tea sets while chatting politely with Abigail and herself. He appeared genuinely interested in their work, the teas and the special cocktails.

Not long after she and Alison had finished hanging the balloons, Susanna marched over to the bar and addressed her stepson.

"I hope you're being careful with those tea sets, Preston? If there are any breakages, you'll be paying for them out of your own pocket. And I hoped you washed your hands thoroughly before touching anything?"

Lilly tried not to scowl at Susanna. The woman was her client, after all, but there had been no need to question Preston the way she had. He was being very careful with her merchandise, and she was grateful for his help.

"I'm being extremely careful, don't worry. And yes, I washed my hands," he replied, not at all fazed by her rude and abrupt manner. "I like your nail polish, by the way. You've had them done in the team colours for the party?"

Susanna looked a little nonplussed for a second, then obviously realised how ornery she sounded and changed her tune. She held out her hands, giving them an admiring gaze. Navy blue and sky blue stripes made up the main nail bed, with white on the tips. "Well, thank you, Preston. Yes, I thought I'd get my nails done for the occasion."

"They suit you."

"Yes, I know. Well, I think I'll make a start getting the presents from the car."

"Need any help?"

"I'll help," Alison said quickly.

"All right," Preston nodded. "But if anything is too heavy, just give me a shout."

The three of them watched as Susanna and Alison made their way over to a top of the range golf sports car in navy blue with white leather upholstery. Abigail let out a breath.

"Well, I must say you handled that very well, Preston," she said. "I'm not sure I'd have been quite as polite."

"I'll agree with that," Lilly said, grinning.

"Kill her with kindness. That's my cunning plan," he said. "She has never really liked me and I don't suppose I make it any easier dressing the way I do. Maybe I should have gone all preppy just for today and kept the peace."

"I think the goth rock look suits you," Lilly said. "If you can't do it now when you're young, then when will you be able to? It's all about self expression and is important. If you don't mind me asking, Preston, how old are you?"

"Twenty three next. I was really young when dad married Susanna, and spent most of my time away at boarding school, so never really had the chance to get to know her. Once I left school, before I went to university, I was home then for a while and it was a bit of a shock for her. She always seems surprised when I come home for family events for some reason. I would never miss Pete's 16th birthday. She's a great mum to Peter, don't get me wrong, she just doesn't know what to think of me, I suppose."

"It's a healthy and mature way of looking at," Lilly said. "Abigail!" she said suddenly. "When did you learn how to do that?"

"Oh, wow, they're great," Preston added, as they both gazed admiringly at the tri-coloured napkins Abigail had deftly folded into the shape of boats. Hanging the name tags off the stern.

"They really are," Lilly said. "What a perfect finishing touch, Abigail."

Abigail blushed slightly under their appreciation. "Thank you. I'm glad they turned out so well."

She spent a couple of minutes teaching them both how to do the rest. Lilly struggled a little at first, but Preston took to it like a pro and soon enough they were finished. Both Lilly and Abigail were impressed with Preston's willingness to help and his personality as a whole. He really was a nice, polite young man and, so far, nothing had been too much trouble for him. Lilly couldn't understand Susanna's attitude toward Preston. She seemed to pick on him constantly. She understood he'd been away for much of the time when he was growing up, but still, he was her stepson and, as far as Lilly was concerned, she really should treat him better.

The final task was to lay the tables and once that was done, they declared themselves finished.

"And bang on time," Lilly said, checking the time on her phone. "Preston, you've been a huge help. Thanks so much."

"You're welcome. I enjoyed it actually. If you don't need me anymore, I see one of my friends has just turned up."

"No, you go and enjoy the party."

Lilly could see now a queue of cars waiting to come through the gate. It was not a small gathering. There were both youngsters from Peter's school and rowing teams, as well as parents and siblings. The day promised to be a lot of fun. Providing Susanna relaxed and allowed herself to enjoy the occasion, Lilly thought privately.

Chapter Five

SOON, THE CROWDS had all arrived. The gate to the site had been closed with the 'Private Event' sign hung across it, and the party was well underway. Large droves of teenagers were playing Frisbee or football on the surrounding fields. Many more, including families, were out rowing on the lake and there was even an impromptu game of cricket happening on the far side of the boathouse, well away from the water.

Lilly and Abigail were busy pouring wine and beer for the older guests and mixing mocktails for the younger crowd. Some of the small children were given freshly squeezed fruit juice or a healthy smoothie.

A couple of hours of fun and frivolity later Susanna rang the ship's bell attached to the boathouse, signalling the time for the food to be served, and Lilly and Abigail jumped into action.

"You know if we do this kind of event again," Abigail said, having laid her seventh platter of sandwiches on one of the tables. "We need to make sure we have staff with us. This is far too much work for just the two of us."

"I agree, Abigail, but the first thing to confirm is that we are actually catering for the numbers we were given in the first place. I don't know if you've noticed, but there are a lot more people here than we had estimated for. Invitees have obviously thought nothing of bringing their entire families with them."

Abigail looked at the crowds in horrified realisation. "Do you think Susanna knows? What will we do if we run out of food, Lilly?"

"If we do, then we do. We have enough for the numbers given to us. As to your other question, I have no idea. But I will be having a discussion about additional payment for the extra work with her in the coming days."

Abigail nodded. "Yes. I'll be there too, if you don't mind? It's one thing to..." she was interrupted by a loud crash from the picnic table nearest the water.

Lilly jolted, nearly spilling the tea she was carrying. She looked across in horror at the carnage of smashed china, glass and spilled food and drink.

"Are you insane, girl?" Edgar roared, leaping up from his seat at the next table and looming upon the girl responsible. "How dare you show up here and ruin my son's party!"

Lilly didn't recognise her, and was sure she wasn't one of the official guests as it was the first time she had seen her. Suddenly Alison charged over from where she'd been chatting with friends by the lake.

"Victoria! What are you doing?"

Victoria pushed her away. "Don't touch me!" She snapped. "Where's Peter?"

Ah, the ex-girlfriend, Lilly thought, too shocked at the girl's outburst to mourn the loss of one of her tea sets.

"You're crazy!" Alison shouted at the furious girl.

"I am so sorry," Edgar said as he approached Lilly, looking positively stunned. "We'll obviously pay for all the damaged crockery. Please, just add it to the final invoice."

Peter had turned up and was now approaching his ex-girlfriend, wide-eyed and slack jawed.

"Vicky, what the heck are you doing? I know you're angry, but that's no excuse to start breaking someone else's stuff."

He attempted to pull her to one side, away from all the gawping guests, but Victoria was having none of it. She pulled back her arm with the obvious intent of slapping him, but Peter was quick and took a step back, causing the girl to stumble and nearly fall.

"You're a pig, Peter Stapleton!" she shouted. "And you're going to regret *everything!*"

She spun round and stormed angrily away, leaving Peter staring after her with his mouth hanging open and his cheeks red with embarrassment.

Now, what on earth was that *all about*? Lilly mused. She glanced at Preston to find him grinning and shaking his head.

"Wipe that stupid grin off your face, Preston. This is no laughing matter!" Susanna spat at him in front of the increasingly silent crowd.

Preston's colour rose, echoing that of his younger brother, but to his credit, he didn't retaliate. Lilly couldn't help but feel sorry for him.

"How are you doing, Abigail?" Lilly asked, noticing her friend didn't look happy.

"I'll be glad when it's over, to be honest. It started out so well, didn't it? Now it's all spoiled."

"That's families for you, I suppose. There's always a little drama at these sorts of events. Don't worry, I'm sure it will get better."

"Well, it can't get any worse, can it?" she replied with a rueful smile.

But there Abigail was wrong. It could and it did.

WHILE EDGAR STAPLETON had offered to pay for all the broken items, he had made it clear he would be pursuing Victoria's parents for reimbursement. Only fair, Lilly thought, considering it was their daughter who had smashed everything in a fit of pique. But Lilly was left wondering what had happened to make the girl so angry in the first place? Teenage angst she could understand, but this seemed way over the top for a simple boyfriend girlfriend spat.

The party continued, somewhat subdued to start and with a lot of whispers and speculation, as well as darting glances and finger pointing at the hosts, but soon enough, with the sun shining, the cocktails and food flowing, a genuine party and celebratory atmosphere ensued.

Abigail and Lilly continued with their serving and after lunch, while the teenagers made merry on the water and in the fields, they began clearing away and preparing the desserts. Abigail had already made a fine selection at the cafe, so it was a case of setting them out and serving as people wanted them.

Lilly entered the boathouse to get more water for the kettles and saw Peter and his mother standing in a corner, having what looked like a heated argument. Peter looked annoyed and tense, and while Lilly tried not to eavesdrop, it was impossible not to hear what was being said when the boy raised his voice.

"He's my brother, whether you like it or not. To be honest, I'm fed up with him being uncomfortable coming to our house or being with us because you're constantly on his case. You really embarrassed him out there, mum. It was bad form and totally unnecessary."

Susanna laid a hand on his arm.

"I'm sorry, Peter."

"It's not me you need to apologise to, mum, it's Preston," he said, then left the building in search of his friends.

Lilly nodded to herself. She was glad Peter was supporting his brother. Susanna's unfounded and harsh words to Preston had been uncomfortable for her to witness, so goodness knows how Preston had felt.

As she left the boathouse to go back to the outside bar, she spotted Susanna speaking calmly and quite obviously apologetically to Preston. Perhaps the party would continue happily from now on.

Lilly filled and switched on several kettles there was tea to serve with the desserts, and glancing over, the tables were filling rapidly.

"We'd better get our serving skates on again, Lilly," Abigail said, handing her a tray full of Eton Mess in vintage bowls along with an old-fashioned jug full of cream.

At the tables, Lilly heard Edgar whispering to Oscar. He'd somehow ended up sitting between both of Peter's rowing team friends. Quintin was on his other side.

"I'm just thankful we took care of those loose ends."

"Me too," Oscar replied. "Thanks for helping us out with it."

"Anytime," Edgar replied with meaning. "Mark my words, the team will do a lot better this season."

Oscar nodded and immediately picked up his spoon as Lilly placed a bowl in front of him.

"Hey! This looks great, thanks," he said extra loudly, and to Lilly's mind a bit forced, as he tucked into the meringue, whipped cream and fresh strawberry confection with gusto.

She moved on to Edgar, who was speaking softly with Quintin and hadn't noticed her. She was just in time to see the man hand a large amount of folded cash to Quintin, who hurriedly stuffed it in his pocket. She put Edgar's dessert in front of him and watched him jump slightly.

"Thanks for picking up that birthday present, Quintin. There's a bit extra included for your time."

Quintin frowned, then glanced at Lilly and smiled.

"Yes, no problem. Thanks."

Lilly served Quintin his dessert and left them to it. Whatever was going on between them all was clearly not meant for her. But, while it was certainly best that she have nothing to do with it, she did admit a small part of her wanted to know what it was all about.

After the desserts were cleared away, it was time for the cake to be brought out. A fabulous three tiered affair in the club colours with a rowing boat and team as the topper. Susanna had ordered it from The Loafer bakery in town, coincidentally owned by a friend of Lilly's, also called Susanna, and it was superb. With the candles blown out, Happy Birthday sung to a grinning but slightly embarrassed Peter, it was time for the giving of gifts.

The first was a large, long and heavy wooden box tied with a blue ribbon.

"This is from your dad and me," Susanna said. "We thought you might like it."

Peter undid the bow, unhooked the brass clasps and opened the lid. Inside were two antique looking oars nestled on deep blue velvet.

Edgar stood and addressed Peter and the crowd gathered round the table, telling them they had once belonged to Peter's grandfather, who had used them to row to victory in the Oxford-Cambridge boat race. He turned back to his son. "I thought they'd be a good gift for you, Peter."

Peter hugged his parents and nodded. Lilly could tell he was overwhelmed by the present.

"They are, dad. Thank you. I'll take good care of them."

Peter then turned to the other pile of gifts on the table, opening them one by one and thanking the people who'd been so generous. Once the ceremony was over and the cake divided and shared out between the guests, leaving the topper for Peter to keep, the guests once again dispersed to enjoy the rest of the day.

"I THINK WE CAN begin to clear away, Abigail," Lilly said, moving towards the tables.

Abigail glanced at her watch and nodded. "This last hour has sped by, hasn't it? I'm so pleased the drama of earlier has been forgotten. I'm enjoying it again now."

As they worked, both Alison and Preston came over separately to ask if they needed any help, but Lilly assured them they were fine and to go and enjoy what remained of the afternoon. Preston went on to set up a game of croquet, and Alison rejoined the Frisbee team.

About half an hour later, as Abigail was carefully stowing away tea sets in their boxes, and Lilly was emptying the kettles, a voice spoke behind them. It was Susanna.

"They really are such a happy group of teenagers. Today was a great success. Thank you both for all your hard work."

"You're very welcome," Lilly said.

"We've enjoyed it, too," Abigail added. "I must say, those oars were beautiful. Such a wonderful gift."

"That was Edgar's idea. His father was an excellent rower, and I'm sure he'd be thrilled to know Peter has taken up his mantle. It's nice to be able to pass on these heirlooms to the next generation. It means so much more when they stay in the family to be appreciated, rather than to a complete stranger. Don't you agree?"

"Oh, I do," Abigail said. "I have a couple of pieces from my grandmother's jewellery collection I'd never part with. Your son looked very moved by the gift."

"He was. And as long as Peter is happy, then I am happy. And talking of the gifts, I think it's about time I loaded them into the car."

"We've almost finished here. I'll give you a hand," Lilly said.

"That's kind of you, thank you, Lilly. Edgar was going to help, but he seems to have disappeared. And I really must apologise for that silly girl's appalling behaviour earlier. Edgar and I were mortified. I always thought Victoria was such a nice girl, but she really showed her true colours today. It just goes to show you never really know anyone truly, do you?"

It didn't take long for the smaller gifts to be packed into Susanna's Golf, but the box containing the oars was far too big. Susanna decided the best place for them temporarily would be the boathouse. Edgar would collect them in his range rover later.

With the last of their boxes safely in Lilly's car, she and Abigail were just about to find their clients to say goodbye, when there was a loud shriek, followed by a scream coming from the edge of the lake. Lilly's heart lurched and turned to ice. She knew that sound and it wasn't a yell of joy, it was one of shock and terror. Something awful had happened.

BOTH LILLY AND Abigail set off running to the bank where the boats were drawn up and immediately saw Susanna and Preston up to their thighs in the water, dragging a limp body from the lake.

"Oh, no," Lilly cried out, racing down to the water and wading into help. She noted several people were already on phones calling an ambulance, so yelled to Abigail to phone Bonnie immediately. Regardless of whether this was a suspicious death or not, and Lilly suspected it might be, Bonnie would need to know. Any unexplained death was cause for a police investigation, even if it was just to prove it was an accident.

On the bank, Preston had quickly rolled his father onto his back. Checking his airways for any obstruction and finding none, he got to work with cardiopulmonary resuscitation.

Peter scrambled down to the bank crying for dad and was held back by Quintin and Oscar, leaving Preston room to try desperately to save his father's life.

Susanna was in the arms of Alison, who was trying to keep the stricken woman from collapsing. All around, the stunned crowd were in various states of shock. Clutching one other, some crying, others silent while they took in the devastating scene and prayed Edgar would pull through.

But it was apparent after ten minutes of trying valiantly that Preston wasn't going to revive his dad, and Susanna quietly told him to stop just as the ambulance siren was heard and the emergency vehicle pulled into the car-park.

Lilly reached down and took Preston's hand, pulling him up and leading him away from the water and back up the bank. He looked at her with glazed eyes.

"I don't know what happened." He staggered and Lilly caught him, held him up. "Oh, my God, he's dead. My dad is dead."

She half carried and half dragged him back to the picnic tables, where she was both relieved and impressed to see Abigail had set up the kettles again and was serving hot sweet tea for the shock. She saw him safely to a table, where Peter and Susanna joined him moments later, and went to get them a drink. As she gazed across at the crowd, she noticed Victoria standing among them in floods of tears and wondered when she'd returned. Or had she never left?

"Here," Abigail said. "I've got a tray ready for the Stapletons, plenty of sugar."

"Well done, Abigail. I'll take it over, then go and tell the paramedics to wait for Bonnie. She won't want anything moved until she can get here and see the situation for herself."

"Already done. I intercepted them as soon as they arrived and informed them Bonnie was on her way. It's not as though they could do anything for the poor man, so a minute delay wouldn't make any difference."

"Thank goodness one of us is on the ball. Thank you, Abigail."

"You are too, Lilly. I just did it first, that's all. I've worked with both of you long enough to know how things need to be done. Go over and take their tea before it goes cold. We can talk shortly."

"Could you get hold of one of the adults and ask them to make sure no one leaves?"

"Of course."

At the table, where Susanna and Peter were clutching at one another in shared grief, and Preston had hold of his brother's hand across the table, Lilly poured them all tea and added sugar.

"I can't believe dad's gone," Peter said through the tears.

"What happened? Preston, did you see anything?" Susanna asked.

"No, nothing," he said, turning despairing eyes in her direction. "I just looked up and saw him floating face down in the water. That's when I shouted you and we raced in after him."

Susanna shook her head. "I don't understand it. The water is calm and Edgar was such a good swimmer..." She stopped and choked out a sob.

Lilly left them alone and saw a police car pull into the car-park.

"Bonnie has arrived," she said to Abigail. "I'll go and explain what's happened."

Lilly met Bonnie at the water's edge, where she was gazing out at the lake, frowning in concentration.

"Hi, Lilly."

"Hi, Bonnie. It seems I only see you nowadays when something awful happens."

"I know. We're both leading busy lives, but we should make an effort to get together a bit more often." She turned to the body. "Dreadful time to go, on your kid's 16th birthday party. That boy will for ever associate his birthday with the death of his father." She turned back to look out at the lake, spending some minutes in thought.

"Bonnie, is there something on your mind?" Lilly asked.

"Edgar Stapleton," she said. "I didn't know him personally, but I've heard of him. Did you know he was an Olympic swimmer, Lilly? Has a couple of bronze medals to his name, too. The family is a high achieving one in the sports world."

"I had no idea. But in that case..."

Bonnie nodded. "What is he, mid to late forties? And with a lake as calm as it is today, unless he had a stroke or a heart attack, I don't think he drowned."

"And he's fully clothed. What was he doing in the water in the first place? He obviously wasn't swimming. Maybe he was in one of the boats and fell out? But I don't remember seeing him out there."

Bonnie sighed. "Lilly, I don't think this was an accident."

Chapter Six

LILLY HAD SPENT a leisurely Sunday with Archie, walking hand in hand around a nearby village and stopping for lunch at one of the best pubs in the area. She'd brought him up to date with what had happened at the party and, understandably, he was concerned. Not only for the family and the guests who had been present, but for Lilly herself.

"I've never known anyone to attract crime like you do, you know. It beggars belief, it really does. I don't think I'll bother with anymore investigative work. All I need do is tag along with you every day and the crime will come to me. What's it doing to your mental and emotional state, though? That's what I'd like to know?"

"Why? Do I seem a little off my rocker?" she'd replied, grinning.

"No more than usual. But I'm used to that. It's part of your charm."

She'd laughed and assured him she was actually fine and coping.

"I'm seeing Dr Jorgenson regularly, which is a great help. And being able to talk things through with you, Archie, means everything. It stops me from brooding."

"I'll always be here for you, Lilly," he said matter-of-factly. "For as long as you'll have me."

She was still feeling the warm glow of that conversation on Monday morning as she tidied the shop in readiness for opening, and found herself wearing a goofy grin more than once.

"Get a grip, Lilly," she said to herself. "You're not a teenager." Which made her think of the party and the traumatic end. She felt a bit guilty then for being so happy.

She cast a discerning eye around the shop, checking everything was in order, before turning the sign to open and unlocking the door. She was on her own this morning, as Stacey was at college. She'd hardly got back behind the counter when the door banged opening and a customer rushed in. Dripping wet and shaking a ruined umbrella.

"Oh, Charlotte," Lilly exclaimed, rushing forward. "Let me take your coat. I'll hang it up by the radiator to dry. Would you like some tea? I have the lemon lavender on the go at the moment, but I can do you something else if you'd prefer?"

Charlotte Hearn was a Plumpton Mallet resident and a regular at Lilly's shop. In her middle fifties, she'd been a primary school teacher before a substantial lottery win had seen her take early retirement. Now she and her husband dedicated their time between child literacy and homelessness charities in the UK, and humanitarian works abroad.

"Lemon lavender is fine, Lilly, thank you. And could you ditch this infernal brolly for me?"

Lilly nodded, taking the mangled piece of fabric and twisted wire. "What on earth happened to it?"

"Got caught in a strong gust of wind and blew inside out. I was nearly Mary Poppins there for a minute, being dragged all over the pavement. I don't know why I just didn't let go of the stupid thing. There's an absolute squall blowing outside. I thought it was too early for April showers. Just proves I know nothing about the weather."

Lilly poured Charlotte a cup of tea and slid it across the counter.

"I suppose you've heard about what happened to Edgar Stapleton?" Charlotte asked Lilly, taking a sip of tea and sighing in satisfaction.

"Unfortunately, Abigail and I were there. We'd been hired to cater his son's sixteenth birthday party at the rowing club."

"Oh, Lilly, how awful for you both to witness! My heart really goes out to that poor family."

"How did you find out, Charlotte?"

"I telephoned Susanna yesterday. I don't know her all that well, but she has some items she was donating to one of my charities. It was the eldest boy, Preston, who answered. He told me. I didn't chat, obviously, just passed on my condolences and said if they needed anything to call. The poor boy sounded absolutely shattered. It just goes to show you must make the most of every day. You just never know when your time will be up."

Lilly nodded in agreement. "So, did you come in for something particular, Charlotte? Or were you just getting out of the rain? It's fine either way, of course. I haven't seen you for a while."

"We've been away. That's why I've not been in recently. I've actually come for a tea set. It's my brother- and sister-in-law's silver wedding shortly. I thought it would be a nice gift for them. Are these your latest ones?" she asked, indicating the beautiful display Stacey had put together.

"They are. But if there's nothing in the shop you deem suitable, I have a catalogue you can have a look through."

Charlotte hopped off the stool and began to peruse the sets. "I can usually find what I'm looking for in your shop, Lilly. This one is gorgeous." She pointed to the cabbage rose design. "I think I'll take it. And I'll have a set of six linen napkins and these silver napkin holders to go with them. Better have something silver, considering the occasion. Could you gift wrap them for me?"

"Yes, of course. Do you want to choose the paper from the display while I box up the set?"

She chose a white and silver vintage design and Lilly deftly wrapped the gifts.

"Do you want me to post them?"

Charlotte shook her head. "No, thanks, Lilly, we're going to the party, so we'll take it with us. I'll have some of the lemon and lavender tea for myself as well, please."

With her purchases carefully stowed in a large, robust bag with The Tea Emporium logo on the side, Charlotte put on her now dry and warm coat, bid Lilly farewell and left the shop. The rain and wind had abated, but the weather forecast had said to expect it on and off for most of the day. Lilly doubted she'd have many customers as a result, so took the opportunity to dust the shelving and the displays.

An hour later, the bell above the door tinkled and in walked Archie. Lilly could immediately tell from the look on his face that he had news.

"HELLO, HELLO, HELLO," Archie said by way of greeting.

He took off his trilby, shaking the droplets outside before closing the door, approached Lilly at the counter, and leaning over gave her a lingering kiss which made her toes curl.

"Now that's what I call a greeting, Mr Brown."

"I aim to please, Miss Tweed."

"So, what's on your mind, Archie?" Lilly asked, pouring him a cup of tea. "I can tell you've found out something important."

"You can read me like a cup of tea leaves."

"I don't read tea leaves, Archie."

"Could be a good little earner to go along with the shop, you know? I can see it now, 'Madam Lilly, Tea and Tasseomancy.' You could have a little fortune tent in the corner over there, and train Earl to sit on your shoulder for added authenticity."

Lilly laughed. "You're a little nuts, you know that, Archie? And what on earth is Tasseomancy?"

"The art of reading tea leaves."

"You know, considering my vocation, I should be familiar with that word, but I'm not. How on earth do you know it?"

"Do you remember in the seventies when the traveller's, or gypsies as they were known then, used to come to your gate selling their wares? They offered fortune telling as well. I was only a boy, but remember my mother getting hers done. I learned it then. It's one of those wonderful words that sticks in your memory. There was a lot of fear in those days of curses if you didn't at least buy something from them. Our pantry was full of more wooden pegs than we had clothes. I used to paint them up to look like soldiers."

"I learn something new about you every time we speak, Archie. So, back to the twenty-first century, what have you found out?"

"I contacted my friendly pathologist. Apparently Edgar had alcohol in his system, not surprising as he was at a party, but, and this is the interesting bit, there were also drugs found. Marijuana laced with something else. Not sure what, but it was obviously potent stuff." Lilly was speechless. Archie nodded grimly. "Bit of a shock, isn't it? The post-mortem isn't complete yet, so I need official confirmation, but that's the news so far."

"I can't believe it of Edgar Stapleton, Archie. I thought he was health conscious considering his history as an athlete? But if he had drugs and alcohol in his system, perhaps it was an accident? I mean, at the very least, his reactions would have been impaired."

"Yes, they would..." Archie mused.

"But?"

"But I honestly don't think there was enough of either in

his system to cause a man with his swimming experience to drown in water as calm as that lake was on Saturday. Bonnie is obviously launching a full investigation, and while they haven't officially said it was murder, I'm leaning toward the fact it was and I think she is as well."

Lilly nodded. "I suppose it does look suspicious when you put all the facts together."

The shop door opened and Lilly looked up to find the last person she expected to see entering. Susanna Stapleton.

"SUSANNA. I DIDN'T expect to see you today. I'm so sorry again about what happened. How are you?" Lilly said, approaching.

She looked a far cry from the perfectly made up and coiffed woman she'd taken on as a client. It had been less than forty-eight hours since Edgar had died, but Susanna had aged years in that short time. So much so she was barely recognisable. Her face was pale and drawn and cosmetic free. Her hair was severely pulled back in a messy bun and the beautiful nail varnish she'd had done especially for the party was chipped and flaking.

Susanna shook her head, close to tears. "I still can't believe it. It's such a shock." She sighed, heavily. "Anyway, I came to settle the rest of the bill."

"There's no need to worry about that now."

"No, I insist. I don't want to have it hanging over me along with everything else."

"Of course, I understand."

"Edgar wrote a cheque at the party just before... well, it includes the cost of what Victoria broke."

Lilly would have been quite happy to cover the cost considering the circumstances, but she could see Susanna had made up her mind and she could hardly argue with a newly bereaved widow. So she took the proffered cheque with thanks and handed her a box of tissues.

"Thank you," Susanna sniffed. "I'm fine, really. I can't think about myself. I need to be strong for Peter. He's not coping at all well. He won't eat or leave the house. He misses his father dreadfully." As she spoke, Susanna was wandering around the shop. She stopped at the latest display.

"It's a terrible thing for a son to lose his father," Lilly said. "How is Preston coping?"

"How much is this set?"

Lilly frowned, wondering if Susanna had deliberately ignored the question or if she'd been so lost in her own thoughts she hadn't heard her. She leaned over and checked the price tag, showing it to Susanna, who nodded.

"And this one?"

Again, Lilly showed her the price on the little tag and Susanna said she'd buy it. Lilly went to see if they already had a boxed set in the storeroom but discovered the only one they had left was the one on display. She explained this to Susanna.

"Can I still buy it?"

"Yes, of course. It will take a little time to pack it up for you, though."

"That's fine, I can browse."

Lilly glanced at Archie, who was already on his feet

with the intention of helping, a bemused look on his face. Together, they transferred the individual items to the counter and began carefully wrapping each piece in tissue paper and transferring them to the box. Lilly kept a concerned eye on Susanna, who was perusing all the high cost items, but seemingly in a daze.

"I'll take these as well," she said, putting two wooden boxes of rare tea on the counter. "Peter is devastated," Susanna said, continuing the conversation where she'd left off. "He won't be going back to school for a while. I had to take his dinner to his room last night. He didn't even touch it. We just sat on his bed together and cried."

Lilly thought again about asking how Preston was, but was stopped when Susanna's mobile phone rang. It seemed it wasn't good news. Archie and Lilly rushed over when she broke down in tears and guided her to one of the stools at the counter.

"I can't believe it!" Susanna raged, slamming her fists on the counter.

Lilly and Archie exchanged shocked glances over head. What on earth had happened now?

"SUSANNA, WHAT'S HAPPENED?" Lilly asked, concerned as the woman continued to rail about injustice.

"That was the solicitor. Edgar has left all his money to Preston! Peter and me get nothing. How could he do that to us? I was his wife! Peter was his son! What about us?"

Suddenly she launched herself from the stool, snatched her handbag from the counter and staggered to the door, knocking over a display of tea as she went.

"Well, we'll see about that," she said, suddenly furious. "I'm not having it. After everything I've done for him, how dare he treat us like this!" She wrenched open the door and slammed it in her wake. Leaving the items she'd wanted still sitting on the counter, beautifully wrapped and unpaid for.

"Good grief," Archie said. "Never a dull moment in The Tea Emporium, is there?"

"Some days I wish I'd never got out of bed."

"Come on, I'll help you tidy up."

They spent half an hour clearing up the mess Susanna had made, and putting back the items she obviously no longer wanted, if she ever really had in the first place, then Lilly made a pot of Ginseng and Ashwagandha blend to help alleviate some of the stress and anxiety Susanna's visit had caused.

"That was a surprising revelation about Edgar's will," Archie said.

"I know. I wonder why he did that?"

"There must be a rational explanation, Lilly. Edgar Stapleton struck me as a man who never did anything without a jolly good reason. Alternatively, it could all be a mistake."

"I feel sorry for Peter, in particular. He idolised his dad."

"I'm sure his older brother will see him right, if what Susanna said is true." Archie said. "It's quite feasible that she got hold of the wrong end of the stick, you know. She wasn't exactly rational when she arrived."

"I wonder how Preston is? I never got an answer from his step-mother. He was the one who fought so hard to save

Edgar's life. It must have been incredibly traumatic, especially considering it was all in vain. I hope he's getting help and support from somewhere because it's obvious he's not getting any from Susanna."

Her phone chimed, and she looked at the message. It was from Stacey apologising that due to some extra college work she wouldn't be able to make it in and hoped that was all right?

Lilly replied, assuring her it was fine and that due to the foul weather, the shop was quiet. Especially now Susanna had left, she thought wryly.

"I better get back to the office," Archie said. "Crime stories to write. Unless you need me?"

"No, I'm fine, Archie, thanks."

"All right, I'll see you tomorrow. It's a midnight oil burning sort of evening, I'm afraid."

"The only thing I'll be burning are the fabulous new soy wax melts I've just got from Cera Scents, while I enjoy a long soak in the bath."

"Sounds wonderful. Are they a new thing?"

"To me they are. I heard about them from a customer and had to try them. You won't believe the gorgeous scents they make. And they are handmade and natural."

"Sadly, I have work to do, but perhaps I'll join you next time," he said with a cheeky wink.

"You'll need an invitation, Archie Brown," she called after him as he opened the door.

"I'll expect one in the post forthwith."

Lilly spent the remainder of the afternoon dealing with just a handful of customers. Margery, a regular, came in to stock upon the lemon and lavender blend of tea, which she was also purchasing as gifts for friends. And a new customer, an elderly man looking for a wedding present for his daughter, bought the tea-set which Susanna had abandoned.

Two minutes before closing time, she scooped up a sleepy cat from the window and put him in his carrier. With a quick look outside and finding no last minute customers dashing across the square to her shop, she locked up and went home.

Chapter Seven

THE NEXT MORNING, apart from the fresh smell in the air and the extra vibrant greenery, all signs of the incessant rain from the previous day had vanished. With the warmth of the sun and everything washed clean, Lilly decided it was a perfect day to cycle into work. She placed Earl's carrier in the basket, which elicited loud and pleasurable purrs from the cat, and set off along the riverside path from her cottage, through the park and up the hill into town.

She had a meeting with Abigail at the cafe later to go through the figures and stock left over from Peter Stapleton's party.

At the shop, she found Stacey was already there and waved through the window. Stacey let her in.

"Morning, Lilly. Good morning to you too, Earl," Stacey said, as the cat, now free from his carrier, wound his way round her legs in a figure eight, positively vibrating with ecstasy.

"I think he missed you," Lilly laughed.

Earl's meows were getting louder and louder as he demanded attention.

"Oh, is your mommy not feeding you?"

"Don't listen to him. He's the best fed cat in Plumpton Mallet."

Stacey scooped him up and took him into the back room, and gave him a spot of breakfast.

"A little extra won't hurt," she said, walking back into the shop.

"He'll get fat," Lilly said.

Stacey grinned. "Don't worry, I won't let him. Second breakfasts are a thing, you know."

"Only if you're a hobbit."

Stacey laughed, then her face turned serious. "So, tell me about the birthday party. I heard Peter's father died?"

Lilly nodded, retrieving the float for the day from the safe and putting it in the old-fashioned till on the counter. "It was a terrible shock for everyone."

"Poor Peter," Stacey said. "What about his mom? How is she?"

Lilly thought about it and eventually said, "A bit unbalanced, if I'm honest. Throughout the party she doted on Peter, yet took every opportunity to belittle his half-brother Preston. It was shameful behaviour, especially in front of a crowd of peers and family friends. Then she came into the shop yesterday to settle the bill. Archie was here, thank goodness, because she received a call from her solicitor with bad news and was livid."

"What news?"

"Obviously, this is between you, me and the gatepost, Stacey, but apparently Edgar left all his money in his will to Preston."

Stacey's eyes widened. "Wow, really? I think I'd be mad, too. What did she say?"

"Burst into tears, then railed about the injustice of it. Said she wasn't going to stand for it. Stomped out of the shop, knocking over the tea display on her way out, and slammed the door. I've put it down to a combination of grief and shock. People act differently when having to deal with such trauma. Archie thinks it's possible she may have misheard the solicitor and jumped to the wrong conclusion."

Stacey nodded. "I hope it all works out for them." She glanced up at the large double-sided railway station clock. "Time to open up."

There was a steady stream of customers in the shop during the morning, the sunny weather bringing everyone out to enjoy it. Stacey and Lilly were kept busy serving tea and boxing up orders, several tea sets included, two of which were to be sent abroad. The lemon and lavender tea was still a best seller and Lilly made a note to blend even more than she had recently, and to pick up from Abigail what was left over from the party.

At lunchtime, Stacey popped down to the cafe and brought back Abigail's special of the day; Spring Orzo with Asparagus, Lemon and Dill.

"Wow, this is fantastic," Lilly said, tucking in. "Abigail is working miracles with the cafe menu."

"I know, it's great, right? This was the vegan option, but she added Feta for us. I could eat this every day." Lilly agreed with her.

A couple of hours later, Lilly left Stacey manning the shop while she strolled further down the market square to the cafe. Inside, Fred was working at the counter and poured her a cup of tea. "Abigail's in the office."

"Thanks, Fred."

Abigail was surrounded by paperwork and tapping away on her laptop when she entered. They always had meetings after any event in order to keep track of costs and inventory. They obviously needed to make a profit, and this one was the first joint venture for the cafe and the tea shop. It would give them a good idea of whether they had got the prices right. She'd learned the hard way, having done a tea tasting event where she only broke even, that even if an event appeared to be a success when it came down to the brass tacks of money, business wise, it wasn't always the case.

"How did we do?" she said, sitting across from her partner.

"It was a success financially, thank goodness, but emotionally I'm drained," Abigail replied.

"You're not the only one. I'm still reeling from how it all ended. Do you have all the paperwork handy? Susanna came in with the cheque yesterday, and I just want to verify it all."

Abigail shuffled through the papers and handed her the relevant sheets. Lilly perused them, but stopped short on the second page.

"Look at this," she said, pointing to a line halfway down the page. "According to these figures, I'm one full crate short of my new tea blend. That can't be right."

"It is. I've been through everything three times. We didn't leave one at the club by accident, did we?"

"No, I made sure to go round everywhere and double check before we left."

Lilly thought back to the day. It had been a whirlwind of activity after Edgar had been found and she and Abigail had packed up and taken everything to the car themselves. It wasn't an issue, but had taken a while.

"Wait a minute," she said. "We left the car unattended once, at the end, with all the doors and boot open. I remember seeing Victoria around there at the time."

"The girl who threw a tantrum at Peter and broke all the glassware and china?"

"Yes. She'd been standing close to the car, then hurriedly walked away. You don't think she took my tea, do you?"

Abigail shrugged. "I've no idea. But honestly, after the way she acted, I wouldn't be surprised to learn she had."

"What on earth would she want with my tea?"

"Haven't the foggiest, but we need to find it or the books won't balance. And you know how I hate loose ends. Or loose tea in this case."

Lilly smiled. "I don't suppose you have the contact details for her family, do you?"

"No, I'm afraid I don't. They weren't invited, were they? But... hang on, I think I know who might have it." She picked up her phone and sent a couple of messages. A quick reply put a smile on her face. "Got it. I'll forward it to your phone."

Lilly glanced at the address but it was unfamiliar to her, so put it into her GPS. "I'll have to drive over. I think I'm grasping at straws a little. I can't see why a teenager would pinch my tea, but if she didn't, we're back to square one. I'll let you know how I get on."

Back at the shop, Lilly brought Stacey up to date, then took her bike and cycled home for her car.

THE GPS DIRECTIONS took Lilly to a brand new estate full of large, detached, four-bedroom family homes a couple of miles on the north side of Plumpton Mallet. Built from local quarried stone with slate roofs and an extended part clad in cedar, they faced south to make the most of the weather and surrounding views of the countryside.

Lilly parked on the opposite side of the road and looked at the house. There were no signs of life and no car in the driveway. She didn't have a phone number to call. She sighed. What a waste of time. She leaned forward to start the engine when she saw the front door open and Victoria came out. She locked the door and was halfway up the path when Lilly jumped out of her car and intercepted her at the top.

"Victoria?"

"Yes?" she said, holding her backpack tighter and giving her a wary look. Lilly could see a free student bus pass in her hand.

"Do you remember me?"

"No. Should I?"

"I own The Tea Emporium in town. I catered Peter's birthday party at the rowing club. It was my tea set you destroyed." Victoria turned pale.

"I'm sorry."

Lilly thought she sounded sincere, but she didn't know the girl. Just because someone apologised, it didn't mean they meant it. She decided to confront her about the tea.

"I'm also here about a crate of my tea that went missing."

"That wasn't me."

Lilly knew instantly the girl was lying and called her bluff.

"I know it was you. I saw you by the car. Why did you take it?" Lilly spoke gently, with no anger. She just wanted the truth, and if possible, her tea returned.

"Because I thought it would ruin the party and Peter's mum would have to pay for it."

It was on the top of Lilly's tongue to ask why she wanted to ruin the party, but thought better of it. It was nothing to do with her.

"Do you still have my tea?"

Victoria nodded.

"Can I have it back, please?"

Victoria disappeared into the house for a moment and returned with the crate. Lilly took it but didn't move.

"Is there something else you want?" Victoria asked. "I'm going to miss my bus to school. I've got netball practice tonight."

"Actually, I do have some questions. I'll give you a lift to school and we can talk on the way. Is that all right?"

Victoria thought about it for a moment, then shrugged and nodded.

"Okay. It's the grammar on the moor road."

Chapter Eight

"SO, YOU USED to be part of the rowing team?" Lilly asked, reversing into a random drive and turning back the way she'd come.

"I was until Peter made me leave."

"Peter did?" Lilly asked, surprised.

"Yes. And we were going out at the time. Pretty humiliating," she said, folding her arms and turning to stare out of the window.

"Why would he do that? I got the impression you were a great rower."

"I was good, but I made a few mistakes and Oscar kept getting at me about it. Said I was letting the team down, which only made me worse. But I could have handled it if Peter had been on my side, but he wasn't. He knew Oscar was upsetting me and what he said wasn't even true, but he never stuck up for me. Not once."

Lilly and Stacey had both been on the receiving end of Oscar's little jibes. He'd come across as a bit of an entitled and privileged chauvinist, but Lilly was surprised to hear Peter hadn't supported Victoria.

"Peter didn't back you up at all?"

"Nope. Then I got angry and lost my temper in front of everyone. Peter was embarrassed, and I'm sure I heard Oscar telling him to kick me off the team. I wouldn't be surprised if he told Peter to dump me, too. I might not be the best in the team, but I really tried, and I was improving. The least Peter could have done was to stand up for me. Anyway, Peter called me the night of the argument. I thought he was calling to see how I was doing, but he'd phoned to kick me off the team and to break up with me." Victoria sighed, and Lilly could see in the quivering of her chin she was still very upset about what had happened.

"I'm sorry. What did you do?"

"I tried to talk him round. I accused Oscar of poisoning Peter's mind, having some sort of hold over him, but he denied it. Told me I was seeing things that weren't there. He said the decision was his, and he was going to break up with me and ask me to leave the team, anyway. Even before I'd shouted at him. I didn't believe him. I know he did it on Oscar's say so."

Lilly tried to make sense of what she was hearing. Peter had stood up to his mother about the way she'd treated Preston. Why wouldn't he do the same for his girlfriend?

"How did Alison feel about it?" she assumed the girls would stick together. She glanced at Victoria and saw she'd turned a deep shade of scarlet. She shifted gear and turned the corner onto the town's main street, staying silent while she waited for Victoria to answer.

"Look, I'm not proud of this, and really regret it now, but during the argument with the Peter in front of the team, I ending up slapping her. I wasn't thinking straight at that point and was convinced she was in on the plan to get rid of me." The girl's voice eventually broke as she continued. "We were best friends. Have been since infants school. The next day I called her and apologised, explained I thought Oscar was to blame and she asked me what proof I had. I told her what I thought I'd heard him say. She told me I was making it all up and spreading lies about her team mates. She said she was glad I wasn't on the team anymore. I told her to watch out for Oscar, that he couldn't be trusted and he'd come for her next, but she refused to believe me. We ended up yelling at each other. We haven't talked since." Victoria sniffed and wiped the tears from her cheeks.

Lilly couldn't help but feel sorry for her. At the age she was, the loss of her boyfriend, her best friend, and the membership of the rowing team would seem like the end of the world.

"Why do think Alison didn't believe you? You were both friends long before Peter and the others came on the scene."

"I think she wants to stay on Peter's side because she fancies Preston. She's always asking Peter about him and she was hanging around him at the party. She didn't stick up for me with Oscar and didn't believe me when I said he was manipulating Peter. Maybe she supported our breakup too? I don't know. I don't know what to do."

They'd arrived at the school. Lilly parked across the road and, pulling on the handbrake, turned to Victoria.

"My advice would be to keep apologising to Alison, explain how much you regret what you did, but more importantly, tell her how much you miss her friendship. You miss her. Give it a few weeks. I know that sounds like a long time, but it really isn't, Victoria, and it will be nothing more than water under the bridge. Alison will either choose to forgive you or she won't. But either way, you will know in your heart you've tried your best to make amends for what you did. I hope she will see that. I also hope that at some point in the future, you and Peter can be friends. There may not be any romance, but life is too short to make enemies of good people, Victoria. Edgar's sudden death proves that."

Victoria nodded and gave Lilly a wan smile. "Thanks. I'm sorry about your tea. I shouldn't have taken my frustrations out on you, you had nothing to do with it."

"Don't worry about the tea, I've got it back and I understand why you did it. Just don't do anything like that again, okay?"

Victoria nodded and got out of the car. Giving a quick wave before running across the road and into the school grounds. Lilly glanced at her watch. She needed to get back to the shop to help Stacey close up.

At home that night, she was just settling down to read before going to sleep when she received a text message from Abigail. Apparently, there was going to be a small memorial service for Edgar at the rowing club. Considering how angry Susanna currently was at her husband due to the will, she wondered who was organising it? Before turning out her light, she made a mental note to go to the club the next day to find out.

Chapter Nine

THE NEXT DAY, with Stacey willingly holding the fort at the shop and looking after Earl, Lilly drove to the rowing club. She'd hardly known Edgar, but since the party she'd found herself becoming more invested in the family and the future of the two boys.

As she parked up and got out of the car, she could see there were several school teams already going through their paces on the lake. Inside the clubhouse she found an elderly woman cleaning the glass belonging to one of the display cases.

"Hello," she said with a welcoming smile. "Can I help you?"

"I was hoping to find some more information about Edgar Stapleton's memorial service. Can you help?"

"Oh, now wasn't that such a shock? To lose such a dear man in his prime like that is simply tragic. I could hardly believe it when I found out. It's a dreadful loss for the club. Were you there when it happened?"

Lilly nodded.

"You poor thing. I heard it was his heart. Such a shame. You never know when your number will be called, do you? Now, if you give me a moment to boot up the computer, I'll get the details for you. It's old and temperamental, so it will be a little while. There doesn't seem to be much funding available for this sort of thing at the moment. Are you able to wait?" Lilly nodded. "I do know it's being held here tomorrow. I'm Clara Bancroft, by the way."

"Lilly Tweed."

"It was Mrs Stapleton's suggestion, I believe, to hold it here. Edgar was heavily involved in the club. It's a fitting idea, don't you agree?"

"I do."

"Perhaps you'd like to take a look around the displays while you wait? There's a lot of club history here. The trophies, photos of the winning teams, that sort of thing. Then there's much about the lake itself and the house that is now at the bottom. Do you know about that?"

"Yes, actually I looked it up on-line a few days ago. It's a fascinating story. I think I will, thank you. I've not looked around before."

The cabinets were set around the walls of the inside bar and Lilly started with the first on her left, intending to work her way round to one that looked more important than the others, with its own spotlight showcasing numerous articles, medals and cups.

Lilly perused the displays with interest, especially the photographs of the house before it had been flooded. Eventually, she got to the larger display and discovered it was dedicated to Edgar Stapleton. Medals for his Olympic achievements, with a sign saying they were on permanent loan from the family. Numerous photographs of him shaking hands with both local and national celebrities and fellow sports people. And many newspaper and magazine article interviews with him. Edgar was clearly the club's most well-known member and probably was responsible for much of its success. She was so engrossed she didn't hear the person behind her until a hand tapped her shoulder. She whirled round, expecting to see Clara, but came face to face with Lady Defoe instead.

"LADY DEFOE," LILLY said. She was dressed from head to toe in black, and Lilly noticed her eyes were tinged with sadness as she turned to the display case.

"Poor Edgar. What a dreadful way to go."

"I'm so sorry for your loss. Were you very close?"

"Not until very recently, and not what you would call close, no. I'm closer to Preston."

"Well, he is your nephew," Lilly said without thinking.

"Ah, I see the rumour mill has been working again. Yes, he's my nephew and I adore him. Look, Lilly, considering you already know about Preston, I'd much rather you hear the truth from me. I doubt what you've heard through the gossip is wholly correct. I'll see if I can persuade Clara to rustle us up a pot of tea, shall I? It's a bit early for the bar to be open. More's the pity."

Lilly agreed and was sure Lady Defoe would have no problem enlisting Clara's services as a tea lady. She was right, shortly after they both returned, with Clara willingly carrying a tray.

"Shall I be mother?" Lady Defoe asked and began to pour without waiting for a reply from Lilly, who was feeling amused at the turn of events. "Now, where was I? Oh, yes, Preston. He's coping remarkably well, considering what happened to his father and his own courageous attempt to save him."

"It must be very hard for him," Lilly said.

"Harder on Peter, I'd say. At least that's what Preston tells me. Preston's main concern is for his younger brother. Which is admirable. What you need to understand is that although Edgar loved his older son dearly, they didn't have an easy relationship. And unfortunately, it was made more difficult by my own parents." She sighed deeply. "I know you're not prone to gossip, Lilly, which is the reason I'm telling you all this. When my sister got pregnant, my parents were absolutely shocked to the core. You can imagine in those days what an out-of-wedlock child meant. Scandal, the loss of public standing, shame, family reputation in the gutter, ostracised from their circles. That sort of thing. But with a titled family, it was so much worse. Yes, my family is titled as well as my husbands. It's one of the reasons they were so pleased with our match. I can remember vividly how furious my father was and how upset my mother when they learned the news. The atmosphere in the house was absolutely dreadful for days on end. It was all about their feelings, you see. Of course, my poor sister got the brunt of their ire. She was quite a shy girl and didn't make friends easily. But she was absolutely beautiful. Ethereal almost. She was still a teenager when she met Edgar, and as unworldly as she was, he completely swept her off her feet. He was ten years older than her, which made him seem all the more exotic. It was another black mark for him as far as my parents were concerned, though." She stopped to take a sip of tea, then carefully replaced the cup in the saucer. "Eventually, my parents decided the best course of action was to send her to a convent for unwed mothers in Scotland. There she could give birth and then return home, pretending it had never happened. The idea was to have the child adopted, but Edgar wouldn't hear of his son being given to and brought up by strangers. I didn't think about it at the time being little more than a child myself, but it was a very brave and highly moral thing to do."

Lilly nodded. "To bring up a baby is hard enough in this day and age, but as a single father so long ago, well, it speaks volumes about him. I didn't realise."

"No doubt you heard the version where my parents handed the child over to Edgar and told him to deal with it, then walked away threatening him with all sorts if he ever went anywhere near my sister again?"

"Something like that," Lilly said.

"Sadly, as far as my parents part in it is concerned, it's not far from the truth. My sister returned home without the child, but she was never the same again. The birth had been an extremely difficult one and her health severely weakened as a result. The mental, physical and emotional pain of losing her son took its toll on an already weakened body and, along with fact, she was forbidden to see Edgar ever again, not quite a year later she died."

"I'm so very sorry."

"I believe my parents had a bot of a change of heart after she died. They didn't quite blame themselves, of course, but they did help Edgar financially to enable him to bring up and educate Preston properly, although they didn't want to meet him."

"I understood Preston was sent away to boarding school?"

"Yes. Edgar was doing well in business by then and was in the running for an excellent promotion. One he really couldn't afford to turn down. He was finding it difficult to be available for Preston, and it appeared to be a good solution. He never once mentioned the boy's connection to our family, much to his credit, and of course in a boarding school under the name Stapleton, no one ever caught wind of the fact he was the illegitimate off-spring of my sister."

"Who instigated the contact between you?" Lilly asked.

"That was me. He'd not been far from my thoughts ever since he'd been born. He was my dear sister's son and my last link with her. I never expected a reply, but he wrote back immediately. The next time he came to visit his father, I invited him up to the house. We've been getting to know one another ever since. Despite his odd exterior, which I'm sure he'll grow out of in time, he is a delightful young man. I'm very proud of him."

"And your relationship meant you became closer to Edgar, I suppose?"

"That's right. To all the Stapletons, to some extent, actually. That's why it's so difficult to believe Edgar is no longer with us."

It was on the tip of Lilly's tongue to ask Lady Defoe if she was aware of the contents of Edgar's will, but some sixth sense told her to remain quiet. She made do with thanking her for sharing the story. A second later, Clara returned with a printed sheet. It was the information she'd originally come for.

"SO WHAT BRINGS you to the club today, Lilly?" Lady Defoe asked, rising as Clara took away their tea tray.

Lilly waved the sheet of paper. "I came for details of the memorial service. I'd like to attend."

"Did you know Edgar well?" she asked as they wandered back to the reception area.

"Not really. Abigail and I got to know him and Susanna while we were organising the catering for Peter's birthday party."

Lady Defoe snapped her fingers. "Of course. You catered the event, didn't you? Preston did tell me, but it had slipped my mind. There was no need to bother Clara, after all. I'm organising it. Neither Susanna nor Peter are in any fit state to help, although it was Susanna's idea. So Preston asked me. I was glad to help. That's the reason I'm here, to check the suitability of it being held indoors if the weather is poor. I must say you waited for rather a long time for the information from Clara. I wonder if there's a problem?"

Lilly grinned. "Actually, the computer is archaic and needs warming up, apparently. I wouldn't be surprised if she uses a crank handle. In fact, the whole office is barely out of the nineteen fifties from the quick glance I got."

Lady Defoe laughed. "Not very subtle, Lilly, but I like your style. I'll see what I can do. Although I suspect dear Clara will need some training if I donate a top of the range laptop. She's used to the sort of thing Hewlett-Packard was producing in a garage donkey's years ago. As a matter of fact, I suppose a full office re-model would be far more cost effective. I could do it in Edgar's name."

Lilly smiled. Leave it to Lady Defoe to go above and beyond. Clara would be pleased. They paused in front of a group photo showing the various team members and Lilly noticed Peter, Oscar, Quintin, Alison and Victoria standing in a group showing off their medals.

"They're a very good team. Preston and I have come to watch them train a couple of times. It's a shame Victoria is no longer a member," Lady Defoe said with an indulgent smile.

"I thought she was their weakest link?" Lilly said.

"I don't know where you got that impression, Lilly, but it's not true. She was a strong team member. The only thing she lacked was the confidence to believe in her own abilities. Both girls held their own with the boys. No, if any of them were the weak link, it was Quintin. Unfortunately, the poor boy has noodles for arms. Although I believe he's working on that. Edgar was giving him one-on-one training and I think he was seeing some good results."

They continued through to the door, where Lilly hesitated for a moment.

"What is it?" Lady Defoe asked.

"Actually, I was wondering if you had any catering sorted out for tomorrow? I'd be happy to organise something if not."

"That was to be my next job when I got home. I do apologise for not thinking of you first, Lilly. That was very remiss of me. I'd be delighted to take you up on your offer." She reached into her handbag and brought forth a cheque book in a monogrammed leather case. Scribbling furiously, she tore out a cheque and handed it to a surprised Lilly. "Will this be enough for something a little classy but not too high end?"

Lilly glanced down and started. "Goodness, Lady Defoe, you could get Fortnum and Mason for this amount. It's far too much."

"Yes, I probably could, but they wouldn't do it at such short notice. Consider it a bonus for a last minute booking. Cater for two hundred guests. I'll leave it with you to supply what you think is necessary. I trust your judgment. Now, I need to speak to Clara about the office refurbishment. I will see you tomorrow, Lilly. And thank you for your help. As well as your listening ear."

Lilly thanked her in return, then made her way back to her car.

Chapter Ten

SHE HEARD LAUGHTER as she walked to her car and turned to watch several rowing teams competing out on the lake. Glancing at the bank, she saw a solitary figure also watching the fun and games. It was Preston. She decided to go and see how he was.

She cut back to the track and carefully walked down the bank overlooking a small man-made stony beach. He looked up just before she reached him.

"Oh, hi," he said. "Lilly, isn't it?"

"It is. How are you doing, Preston? I really am so sorry about what happened."

He gave her a bleak look and shook his head. "It's awful. I can't believe it happened. Peter's suffering really badly. So is Susanna. I'm just trying to get my head round it. My dad and me weren't the closest. I was away a lot, but he was my dad and we had just begun to get to know each other properly for the first time in my life."

"Losing a parent is tough at any age, Preston. No matter how close you are. And the circumstances here... well, it's very difficult to process, that's what I'm trying to say. Don't spend too much time alone. It's good to have people to talk to, or to simply be with. Are you here on your own?"

"No, my aunt is inside sorting out some stuff for the memorial."

"Yes, I've just had tea with her. She's asked me to do the catering tomorrow."

Preston nodded. "That's good."

"So Peter couldn't come with you today?"

"I'm not staying there. I'm with my aunt and uncle at the moment. But I can't get hold of him, anyway. I've called Susanna loads of times, but she isn't returning my calls. And Peter's phone got broken last week. Although I'm sure he must have got a new number by now." He frowned.

"Just give them a bit of time. I expect the contents of the will came as a bit of a shock. Especially on top of the trauma of your dad's death. "

Peter stared, shaking his head and giving her a confused look. "The will? What do you mean?"

Lilly blinked. "Susanna was in my shop when the solicitor called. Edgar left all his money to you, Preston."

"What?"

"Didn't you know? I thought Susanna would have told you? I'm so sorry if I've put my foot in it."

Lilly was flabbergasted. Surely Preston had a right to know that he was the sole beneficiary in his father's will? Why on earth hadn't Susanna called to tell him? Or asked Peter to if she didn't want to speak with him? She had assumed the solicitor would have been in touch with him as well, but obviously, judging by Preston's surprise, he hadn't. Perhaps there was a delay for some reason? Besides, she honestly thought the will would have been public knowledge by now, considering Susanna had shouted about it in her shop. She and Archie had heard everything, and she was still shouting about it when she left the shop.

"I don't know anything about it," Preston said now, utterly confused. "Why would dad leave everything to me? Does Peter know? Why haven't they called and told me? I should have heard from someone about by now, the solicitor at least, shouldn't I?"

"I would have thought so, yes, but I honestly don't know the answers to your questions, Preston."

"I'm going to talk to my aunt," he said, suddenly jumping up. "Thanks for letting me know."

"I'm sorry it was such a shock. I think talking to Lady Defoe is a very good idea. Good luck, Preston."

"Thanks," he said and jogged back to the boat house.

Lilly watched him go, then got up and made her way back to the car. Thoughts of Edgar's death, his will and the tension in the family whirling around her mind.

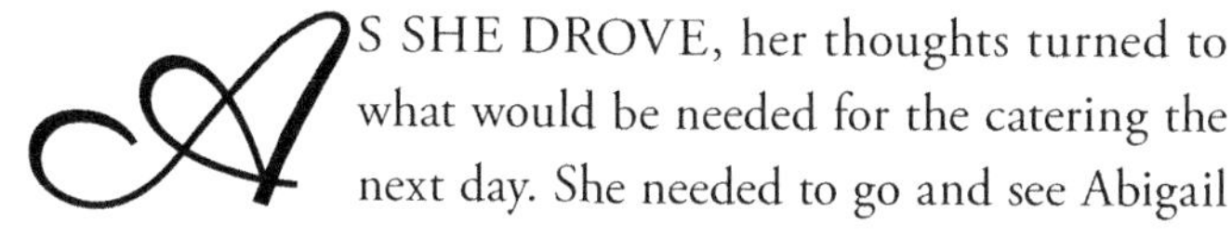

AS SHE DROVE, her thoughts turned to what would be needed for the catering the next day. She needed to go and see Abigail straightaway to inform her. It was short notice, as Lady Defoe had said, but the extra money certainly made it worthwhile. Plus, it was Lilly herself who had offered, so she only had herself to blame if things went wrong.

She was glad she had run into Lady Defoe. She'd certainly learned more about Preston and his father. She couldn't imagine what Preston's childhood had been like. He was so young when his mother had died and then brought up by a father who, while trying to do his best, was obviously finding it difficult. So much so that he sent him to boarding school as soon as he could. Preston had never known or spoken to any of his relatives, yet he had turned out to be a polite, well-balanced young man. Testament to the schools he was enrolled in more than anything else. Perhaps Edgar had left everything to his older son by way of an apology? And probably more than a little guilt, Lilly thought, no matter how misplaced.

She realised she'd been driving on auto-pilot when the heavens opened and large fat spots of rain exploded on the windscreen. She turned on her wipers and after the initial murky spread of dust, the window began to clear.

Her mind turned back to Edgar's death and her increasing feeling that it had been deliberate. She was so caught up in trying to think who could be responsible that she nearly missed seeing the car on the other side of the road, careening round the corner on the narrow, wet, slick road, partially in her lane. She cried out and slammed on her brakes. Turning her wheel left to avoid a collision, she bumped over the grass verge and came to a sudden stop. The front of her car lodged in the hawthorn hedge.

SHE WAS TRYING to catch her breath when there was a rap on the window. It was Peter Stapleton. She wound down the window with a shaking hand.

"Oh my gosh, I am so sorry about that. Are you all right?" the boy said.

"Do I look as though I'm all right? What on earth were you thinking? If that had have been a head-on collision, we could all have been seriously injured if not killed," she said, seeing Quintin and Oscar who'd dashed over the road and stood behind Peter.

"It was my fault," Oscar said, looking pale and frightened. "I lost control on the wet road. I'm really sorry."

Lilly sighed and got out of the car, taking note of the silver Audi A3 parked at the other side of the road. "I didn't know you could drive, Oscar?"

Oscar followed her gaze. "Passed my test a couple of months ago. I'm older than these two. It's my mum's car. I don't have one of my own yet. Listen, you won't say anything about this, will you? She'll go mad if she finds out and I'll be grounded for at least a year and she'll never let me drive again. At least not in her car."

"You were driving too fast, you know?" Lilly said, avoiding an answer. "These are narrow country lanes and you never know what could be round the corner. What if it had been a tractor or a flock of sheep? You need to be more careful. Cars can be killing machines in the wrong hands, Oscar. I hope you've learned your lesson?"

Oscar nodded sheepishly. "I have. Sorry again."

"Can we give you a lift?" Peter said. "I think your car might be damaged."

Lilly looked in dismay at the steam coming out from under the bonnet and shook her head. "Great. Let me call my mechanic, then you may as well take me back to the rowing club, it's nearer than town. I assume that's where you're going?" The three boys nodded. "All right, give me a couple of minutes."

Lilly, very luckily, had a friend who was a mechanic and owned his own garage. Because of the age of her car, she had given him the spare key for moments like this. He said he'd come immediately to pick it up on his low-loader and would also come and get Lilly and take her back to Plumpton Mallet. He'd do his best to get the car fixed and back on the road as soon as he could.

"You're a lifesaver," she said, hanging up and turning to the boys. "All right, I'm ready. But please, Oscar, be careful and stick to the speed limit, would you?"

With Oscar driving and Quintin in the passenger seat. Lilly and Peter sat in the back. It gave her a chance to ask how he was doing. But he shook his head, not wanting to talk. She nodded her understanding.

"We were all close to Mr Stapleton," Quintin said, turning back to face her. "He was our coach. What happened was really awful, but it makes no sense. He was an Olympic swimmer."

"Yeah, well, the police don't think it was an accident," Oscar piped up.

Lilly glanced at Peter. He was staring out of the window, a blank look on his face. But she could see his hands were clasped so tightly his knuckles had turned white.

They arrived back at the rowing club and Lilly noticed Lady Defoe's car had gone, but recognised Susanna's. She must have driven in from the opposite direction.

"Mum's here," Peter said. "She called me this morning saying she wanted to come and see if everything was all right for tomorrow. I was out with my friends, so said Oscar would drive me and I'd meet her here."

Lilly nodded, wondering why he was explaining this to her. She also grasped the fact that Peter had a phone. So why hadn't he called his brother?

Peter loped towards the building, shoulders hunched, while Oscar and Quintin stayed outside for a while, sheltering from the rain under the trees, obviously not wanting to interrupt things inside.

"I hear your team is expected to do really well in the competitions this year?" Lilly said.

Oscar grinned. "Yeah, we've been training really hard."

"And I was doing some extra training with Mr Stapleton," Quintin said. "My stamina has really improved."

"Not like the girls," Oscar scoffed. "Now, me and Mr Stapleton have given them the boot we'll be holding this season's trophy. You just watch."

"Alison is still on the team, Oscar," Quintin said.

"For now. But we both know she's this close to quitting." He held his thumb and forefinger a centimetre apart and grinned. "Right, I'm going in to find Pete and his mum. Um… sorry again about your car and everything," he said to Lilly.

Quintin lingered a moment longer, hands in his pockets and scuffing the gravel with his foot.

"Are you all right, Quintin?"

"Yeah, I'm fine. Just, you know, got stuff on my mind."

"Did you want to tell me something?"

The boy shook his head rapidly. "No, nothing. Just thinking, you know, that you always expect to see someone you know again, and then one day you find out you won't. It's like that with Coach Stapleton. I can't believe I'm not going to see him again." He looked down, blinking rapidly, then shrugged. "Anyway, I'm glad you're okay after the accident. I'm going inside now. Bye."

"Bye, Quintin," Lilly said, watching him rush to catch up with Oscar. She understood exactly what he meant, but she also knew it wasn't what he intended to say in the first place.

Chapter Eleven

AS LILLY HAD expected, apart from the very sad circumstances, Abigail had been thrilled when she'd learned they had a new catering job, but had been thrown into a bit of a panic when she realised it was the next day. However, true to form, her partner was incredibly organised and had various suitable dishes already available in the cafe's freezers. Miniature Quiches in various flavours, vol-au-vents, sausage rolls, and mini pork pies. Plus a selection of vegetariand and vegan dishes. They would be baked the next day, and sandwiches, salads, pasta dishes and other items made as late as possible, packed up, and taken to the venue an hour before the memorial. This would give them time to prepare and have everything ready to serve once the guests returned from the service.

Lilly's task was a little easier and she and Stacey sorted out what would be needed the morning of the event. They'd opted for plain white napkins with plain silver rings and Stacey was busy threading tiny bouquets of forget-me-nots under each one. Without her own car, they'd be using Abigail's, which was much bigger and newer than Lilly's. And, more importantly, hadn't been forced into a hedge the day before. With everything ready, she left through the back storeroom door and met Abigail outside.

"Golly, Lilly, do you think we've gone a bit over the top?" her business partner said, as she crammed the last of the boxes into the back of the car.

Lilly laughed. "I'm quite sure Lady Defoe had no idea how much her money would buy. But none of it will go to waste. Whatever is left, she'll donate to one of her charities, I expect. Now, have we got everything?"

It was Abigail's turn to laugh. "Lilly, considering the amount we've got in here, if we have forgotten something I seriously doubt it will be missed."

The drive over was lovely, made all the more pleasant because the sun was shining and the fields and hills were dotted with ewes and their new-born lambs frolicking and gambolling in the warm weather.

As Abigail pulled into the rowing club car-park, they could see a number of cars had already arrived.

"I was hoping we would be able to set up without an audience," Abigail said, alighting.

"We will be able to," Lilly said, bending to get the first box from the boot. "These are the family cars and they're probably congregating in the upstairs bar. The bar downstairs is where we will be, and that's off limits until the memorial service is over. I double checked with Lady Defoe."

"Where is the service going to be held?"

"Outside on the patio area. The weather is perfect. If it had been too cold or raining, it would have been held in the foyer. I'll show you when we get inside."

They began to carry the food indoors and were met by Clara dressed in a deep charcoal grey trouser suit, who accompanied them to the room and explained she'd taken the liberty of arranging the tables for the buffet, covering them with tablecloths in the club colours.

"That's a great help, Clara, thank you," Lilly said.

"I thought you could set up your tea and kettles behind the bar, Lilly. All the alcohol will be served upstairs only. Will that be suitable?"

"Yes, it will. It's the perfect spot, actually."

"I'll help to bring your boxes in," she said, disappearing out to the car.

"I'll show you where the service is going to be held, Abigail, before we start setting up."

"Lead the way."

Through a side door, they ventured onto the patio area, where chairs had been lined up in rows of four, either side of a central aisle. At the front, an arch had been assembled from eight large oars, tied at the top with rope, where the Vicar would stand. The view of the lake and green hills behind him. To the side was a large wooden easel, presumably to hold an enlarged photograph of Edgar, and beneath that was a wreath of white roses affixed with a dark blue, light blue and white ribbon. The club colours.

"It's quite beautiful, isn't it?" Abigail said.

Lilly agreed. It was somber without being maudlin. A fitting tribute for a man who had been such a pivotal part of the rowing club and its success.

"I've just got the last box to get from the car, then I'll come and help you set out the food," Lilly said.

It was while Lilly was retrieving the last box of tea that she saw Bonnie walking across the car-park toward her. She also was dressed in a black suit for the occasion.

"Hi, Bonnie. I didn't expect to see you here. Have you come for the service?"

"Not exactly. I'm here in a professional capacity to make sure there's no physical altercation. There's a lot of tension in the family at the moment. Susanna is now under the doctor, who has prescribed sedatives to help her sleep. She's not coping at all well. Neither is Peter. And I wanted to take the opportunity to observe them all. You know we're officially treating this as a murder investigation now?"

"I'd heard there was a possibility. What's happened to make it official?"

"The post-mortem revealed some bruising on the back of Edgar's neck, consistent with someone forcing and holding his head under the water. With the drugs and alcohol in his system, there was no chance he could fight back."

Lilly grimaced. "Any idea who it was?"

Bonnie shook her head. "Not yet, but we're working on it," was all she would say.

LILLY AND ABIGAIL stood and watched the memorial service through the window, both with a cup of tea in hand. It would be unlikely they'd get a chance to have another one for a while.

On the left front row, Susanna and Peter sat together. The adjacent chairs remained empty. Susanna was swaying slightly and weeping softly into a handkerchief, her face hidden by a black veil, while Peter, face tight and pale, clutched her hand tightly. On the other side of the aisle, Preston sat between Lady and Lord Defoe. Lilly noticed he gave his younger brother several concerned glances during the proceedings, but Peter never looked up from his lap the entire time.

In the subsequent rows Lilly assumed were other relatives, then came senior club officials and volunteers, and further back, friends and team members, work colleagues and various acquaintances, and people who just wished to pay their respects to the deceased man. The two hundred attendees Lady Defoe had estimated proved to be on the mark. Finally, standing at the back, were Bonnie and two of her officers. There was also a photographer and a reporter from the Plumpton Mallet Gazette. The only members of the press who had been allowed to attend, and only by an official invitation from Susanna Stapleton herself. Lilly had hoped it would be Archie who would be the paper's representative, but he'd told her he wasn't able to come due to other commitments. And it wasn't really within his remit, anyway.

"You were right about the easel," Abigail said in hushed tones as the window overlooking the proceedings was open. "Although I didn't expect a portrait painting."

Lilly hadn't either. It was a large, obviously professional work, done in oils and mounted in a gilt swept frame. She assumed it had come from the Stapleton's home. In it, Edgar Stapleton was sitting in an armchair, legs crossed, casually dressed in a white button-down shirt, pale blue crewneck sweater and jeans, relaxed and smiling in front of a fireplace with a book on his knee. As though he'd been caught unawares while reading and just looked up as his name had been called. It must have been completed quite a while ago, as he didn't look to be much older than thirty-five. But to Lilly's mind, there was a calculated look in his eye. For all its perceived casualness, it had undoubtedly been meticulously planned.

"I think they are just finishing up," Abigail said, as the prayer ended with a hushed 'amen' from the congregation. "Time to get to work."

For the next half hour, Lilly and Abigail were kept busy serving food and tea to a subdued crowd. Eventually, the conversations turned to fond memories of the deceased and anecdotes were shared. The mood began to lift, and the tone changed to one of celebrating a life rather than mourning a death. But Susanna and Peter stayed seated in a corner together, graciously accepting condolences and talking quietly to themselves.

Lilly saw a familiar face standing to the side of the buffet table, nibbling on a sandwich. It was Victoria, in a conservative black dress and jacket. A moment later, she was pleased to see Alison join her. They spoke for a moment, then with plates full of food ventured outside. Lilly double checked she had no one to serve, and with an approving nod from Abigail, took a tray of tea and followed them.

SHE HEARD THE two girls talking as she elbowed her way through the door.

"I'm really sorry, Vick," Alison said. "I was caught up in it all and didn't know how to get out of it. I shouldn't have sided with them. We've been friends since first school and I should have stuck up for you."

"It's okay. I know what they're like. I'm really sorry for slapping you. I shouldn't have done that."

"Forget it. We've both done things we regret. Let's call it quits and be friends again. I'm done with them. I've decided to leave the team."

"Really?" Victoria said. She looked so relieved that she had her friend back.

"Yes. And I think we should start our own team. What do you think? We'd easily beat the boys. And it would serve them right for underestimating us and being so nasty."

Lilly chose to wander over at that point and set the tea on the table.

"I've brought you both some tea. I noticed you didn't bring any with you."

"Oh, hi," Victoria said, smiling. "That's great, thanks. By the way, I spoke with Susanna and apologised. I'm paying her back for the tea set and the other stuff I broke. It will take a while with my part-time job and chores at home, but I feel better about doing it."

"I'm glad," Lilly said. "I couldn't help but overhear. Are you two setting up your own rowing team?"

Alison looked at her friend, who nodded. Alison grinned. "Yes, we are. I'm so sick of all the testosterone and 'boy's club' mentality on the other team. They made life hell for Victoria, which was really unfair. I get the feeling they want me out as well, especially Oscar, who's taking every opportunity now to say how rubbish I am and how much I'll let the team down and stop them from winning anything. Actually, it's only Oscar saying it, but the others aren't sticking up for me either. Just like they did with Victoria. It's no fun anymore and I find myself dreading coming to practice. I just don't need it."

"Do you mind me asking what happened?" Lilly said, taking a seat.

Alison sighed. "This is probably the worst time and place to admit it, but it was Peter's dad who kept whispering in Oscar's ear, saying girls couldn't hold their own on a team like theirs. Apparently, women aren't strong enough. You know, we're the weaker sex and all that. He thought we were dragging the team down and he really, really, wanted to win."

"Edgar said that?" Lilly asked in surprise. "I thought Oscar was the culprit."

"Oscar is a misogynist through and through," Victoria said. "But it was Mr Stapleton who instigated it. They think the same and he encouraged Oscar's attitude."

Alison nodded. "That's right. They forced Victoria out and they're trying to do the same to me now. I'm fed up with all of it."

"I don't blame you. I'm sorry you were made to feel like that, especially by someone who should have known better."

"You know, we weren't the worst on the team. When Quintin first started, he could barely hold the oars," Alison said. "He would have to stop and rest way before either of us would. But rather than letting him go, Mr Stapleton started doing weight and endurance training with him. It was working too. I asked for something similar once but was made to feel like a lost cause. He was really condescending, actually. I'm not blaming Quintin. He's actually a really nice guy. It's just the way it is."

"I think Mr Stapleton thought that if he replaced us with two strong boys, then his son would have a better chance of being part of a winning team," Victoria said. "He wanted the son of an Olympian to look good. Couldn't have his progeny failing because of two weak girls. What would that do to his reputation and standing with the club?"

Alison nodded. "I never thought of it like that, but you're right. Mr Stapleton loved playing the celebrity, didn't he? Loved all the limelight. He couldn't stand being made fun of or made to look stupid." She paused and look away for a moment. "Wow, it's always been about him really, hasn't it?" and her friend nodded. "Let's not talk about it anymore. We've wasted enough time on them."

"So, who are we going to recruit for our new team?" Victoria said.

"I'll leave you to it," Lilly said, getting up and lifting the tray.

"Thanks for the tea," both girls said before resuming their conversation.

Inside, almost everyone had finished with food and drinks, and Abigail was beginning to surreptitiously pack things away. She caught Lilly's eye and gave a wink. Lilly smiled and began clearing away empty cups and teapots that had been abandoned in various places.

SHE WAS JUST washing some saucers when Abigail sidled up beside her. "You know, I had a thought. Why don't we pack all the crockery away as it is, then we can run it all through the dishwashers at the cafe? It would save so much time, especially considering that sink is about the size of my foot spa. Assuming it's all dishwasher safe, of course?"

"Now, that is a brilliant idea. And yes, it's all safe. This sink is just meant for glasses. Thanks, Abigail," Lilly said, drying her hands on a tea towel.

"They've just opened the book of condolence, are you going to sign it?"

"I think we should, don't you?"

"Yes, I do, actually. We might not have known him very well, but Edgar died while we were here. I think it's only good manners that we pay our respects. You go first and I'll continue to pack up, then we can swap."

Lilly joined the currently small line and found herself directly behind Quintin, who turned and struck up an impromptu conversation with her about his coach. He certainly had nothing negative to say about the man and he clearly thought him a first rate coach and mentor.

"I am sorry for your loss, Quintin. It's obvious how close you were."

"I've not trained since Peter's party. I know I need to get back into it, but it won't be the same without Mr Stapleton's encouragement."

"You will when you're ready," Lilly said. "Just remember, Quintin, Edgar obviously had a lot of faith and belief in you. I'm sure he'd like to know you were keeping up with what he taught you."

"Yeah, I should do it for both of us. You're right. Thanks." He picked up the pen and signed the book, then with a nod at Lilly, he moved away. She wrote a brief note, smiling at Quintin's squiggly, practically indecipherable handwriting, then returned to Abigail.

She spied Bonnie on the periphery of the crowd, tea in hand, observing everyone and everything. She wondered if she was aware of Edgar's fervent desire for an all-boy rowing team and how the girls had been treated as a result? Probably, she admitted. Bonnie hardly ever missed a trick.

Chapter Twelve

THE FOLLOWING DAY Lilly was in the shop early, double checking the new items she'd ordered had actually arrived. She was making a 'to-do' list when Stacey came through from the stockroom.

"The new citrus tea services have definitely not been delivered," she said. "And we're missing the country cottage place mats and coasters."

"I thought that must be the case, as they aren't in the system. You always put new stock into the computer. I had wondered if they'd arrived while you weren't working and one of the others had put it away, not knowing what to do with it?"

Stacey shook her head. "Not this time."

It used to be just the two of them who handled everything in The Tea Emporium, but when Lilly and Abigail had relaunched the cafe under their joint ownership, they had started to train cafe staff to work in the tea shop as well.

Most of them enjoyed being able to work in both places, but no one, apart from Lilly herself, knew the ways of her shop quite as well as Stacey.

"I think some additional training is needed anyway," Stacey said. "If we had two other reliable servers also trained on the inventory side, it would be a great help. We'd know much sooner if stuff hadn't arrived."

"Yes, I agree. Could you make a start on that?"

"I'll add it to my managerial plans for next month. I'll also chase up the missing orders. It's annoying because I have two customers interested in this design and it's making me look like an idiot because I can't show it to them."

Lilly smiled. Making Stacey manager of both the cafe and tea shop had been a good idea. It had given her control of both locations, making it easier to maintain order.

The front door opened and Abigail came rushing into the shop beneath a dripping umbrella. "What is going on with the weather this week? It can't make up its mind," she said, stuffing her folded umbrella into the stand by the door. "Yesterday was beautiful sunshine and not a cloud in the sky. Today there's a monsoon out there."

Monsoon was a slight exaggeration, but Lilly noticed Abigail's favourite suede boots were absolutely soaked through, as was the hem of her skirt just visible beneath the short rain coat.

"I was lucky to get indoors before it started," Lilly said, pouring Abigail a cup of tea.

"I just came downstairs," Stacey said with a grin.

"Lucky you," Abigail said, smiling. "If this weather keeps up, I might just move in with you. Global warming has a lot to answer for. If it carries on like this we'll all have to get boats and row to work. It will be like living in Venice."

"Is everything all right at the cafe?" Lilly asked, wondering why she'd turned up.

"Everything's fine, I just came to bring you this." She pulled a slightly damp envelope from her pocket and handed to Lilly. "It's an Agony Aunt letter. I found it on my desk under some receipts from a couple of days ago. I must have missed it. I hope it's not urgent."

"It was delivered to the cafe?"

"Yes. Odd, isn't it? Most people know this is where they need to be posted. It must be someone unfamiliar with you being Plumpton Mallet's Agony Aunt."

"Well, it is called The Agony Aunt's cafe," Stacey said. "Easy mistake to make, I guess."

Lilly laughed. "Stacey has a point. Perhaps we should have a box over at the cafe, too?"

Abigail nodded. "Not a bad idea. I'll think about it. Although, to be honest, it's no trouble to bring them over here if I do get one. It might just be a waste of money. This is the first one I've ever had."

"I spoke in jest, Abigail. I don't really think there's any need for one at the cafe as well." Lilly said.

"Oh, good. I didn't know how to say it was a daft idea without offending you," Abigail said, breathing a sigh of relief.

But reading the contents of the letter with a sinking heart, Lilly didn't hear her.

Dear Agony Aunt,

I hope you can help me as I have got myself into some trouble and I don't know how to get out of it. I made a mistake. A bad one. I've been taking some steroids to help with my stamina and they caused really bad headaches. I feel like I'm spiraling down and I don't know how to stop. Someone close to me overdosed recently and I think it was my fault. Now I'm frightened because I don't know if I can give up the steroids. I can't talk to my family or friends about it. What should I do?

"Oh dear," Lilly said.

"What is it?" Abigail and Stacey said together.

Lilly showed them the letter. "I know who it's from. I recognised the handwriting straightaway. I need to call Bonnie."

BONNIE WAS AT the station when Lilly called, and as it was just at the other side of the market square, she was walking through the door no more than five minutes later.

"Can you believe the sunshine out there now after the deluge we've just had?" was her greeting.

"That's my cue to leave," Abigail said. "The breakfast crowd will be arriving at the cafe now the rain has stopped. Let me know what you learn."

"You said you had something for me?" Bonnie said, taking a stool at the bar and accepting a cup of tea from Stacey with a nod of thanks.

Lilly handed her the letter. "I know these are supposed to be anonymous, and under any other circumstance, this also would be. But, I recognise the handwriting and the author is still a child. And he's talking about a recent overdose."

Bonnie read the letter, then looked up at Lilly. "Tell me what you know."

"The letter is from Quintin, one of Peter Stapleton's rowing team members."

"The scrawny boy?" Bonnie asked, pulling out her notebook.

Lilly nodded. "Archie told me there were drugs found in Edgar's system during the post-mortem, but those details haven't been made public, so how else would Quintin know about it?"

"You're assuming the person he mentions being close to is Edgar Stapleton?"

"Oh, come on, Bonnie. Do you know of any other recent drug overdoses?"

"All right, no I don't. Go on."

"Edgar was training Quintin personally, and they saw a lot of one another. The boy admired him greatly, almost to the point of hero worship. Archie said there was marijuana found in Edgar's system, but something else as well. Have you identified it yet?"

Bonnie scratched her head and looked away for a moment, debating how much she should say.

"Okay, but this goes no further. As well as the marijuana, there was indication of repetitive abuse of anabolic drugs."

"According to his letter, exactly what Quintin is taking."

"You're sure this is Quintin's handwriting, Lilly?"

"Absolutely positive. He was in the queue in front of me to sign the condolence book at the memorial service yesterday. I recognised it instantly."

"Well, obviously, I have a couple of immediate thoughts. One, that Quintin may have had something to do with what happened to Edgar. And two, who was supplying the boy with the drugs in the first place? I have an idea about that and I expect you do too?" Lilly nodded. "Either way, I need to talk to Quintin immediately. Not least because he's putting his health and life at risk. I doubt very much he knows how damaging these drugs can be."

"Well, I'm not sure I do either," Lilly said.

"I do," Stacey said. "It's one of my degree modules. They can cause what's called 'Roid rage,' you know, extreme aggression, as well as paranoia, delusions, and mania. Long term they can lead to serious and sometimes permanent health problems, like kidney or liver failure, tumours, blood clots, enlarged heart, high blood pressure and they can change blood cholesterol. It means you can end up having a stroke or a heart-attack, even if you're really young. In young people, it can stunt growth and cause all sorts of problems with the reproductive system. They are the worst news. You've got to tell him to stop, Lilly. He's going to ruin his life if he doesn't. Or worse, he could die."

Both Lilly and Bonnie had paled while listening to Stacey.

"Did you know all this?" Lilly asked the detective.

Bonnie shook her head. "Some, but not all of it. I'll make sure he knows the dangers, Stacey."

"Bonnie, would you mind if I came with you?"

"Oh, Lilly," Bonnie groaned. "We've had this conversation before..."

"Yes, I realise that," Lilly said quickly before her friend could utter the 'no,' which was on the tip of her tongue. "But I know Quintin, and he wrote that letter to me. He wants help, Bonnie, or wouldn't have written in the first place, and I want to try to give it to him. I promise I won't get in your way."

"Doesn't Stacey need you in the shop?"

"No, I can manage fine on my own," Stacey said, grinning.

Bonnie rolled her eyes. "Fine. But he's still a child, so if and when this turns into an official interview, his parents will need to be present. At that point, you won't be. Understood?"

"Yes, Ma'am."

Bonnie smiled despite herself. "Less of the cheek. Come on then. We'll treat it as a simple chat to start with, nothing official. I don't want to frighten him."

"Thanks, Bonnie. See you later, Stacey. Thank you for holding the fort. If you need anything, just give me or Abigail a call."

"Will do. Good luck."

"RIGHT," SAID BONNIE, as they got in her car. "The first place to look for him is the school. He should be there at this time of the morning. I'll give the headmaster a call first to check. No point going all the way up there to find he's elsewhere."

Lilly listened to the one-sided conversation and gathered Quintin wasn't due back for lessons until mid-morning.

"So, where is he?" she asked, as Bonnie ended the call.

"The rowing club. They have practice today."

She started the car and a few minutes later was driving out on the country road towards the reservoir. As they reached the crest of the hill the rain started.

"I can't believe this weather," Lilly said. "I never know whether to bring a coat or not."

"There were quite a few traffic accidents because of the wet roads the other day."

"I know. I was run off the road into a hedge."

Bonnie shot her an incredulous look.

"What?"

"Don't worry, I'm fine. Just a bit shaken at the time, but not hurt."

"Why on earth didn't you call me?"

"There was no need. I got a lift to the rowing club. I was coming back from there when it happened, and the garage picked up the car, then came for me and dropped me back in town. You obviously had your hands full anyway. There was nothing you could have done."

"Mmm. Well, let me know next time."

"I hope there won't be a next time, Bonnie."

"Well, yes, of course, so do I."

Lilly had deliberately decided not to mention that it had been Oscar driving the car, with both Quintin and Peter as passengers. Bonnie had enough on her plate trying to investigate the murder without having to deal with a silly accident. She'd given Oscar the hard word, and she was sure he'd learned his lesson. He also knew that if he didn't keep his word and was careful with his driving from now on, then he ran the risk of Lilly telling his parents what had happened. And that he wanted to avoid at all costs. No, she felt sure that telling Bonnie was unnecessary.

When they arrived at the club, the rain had thankfully reduced to a drizzle. They could see several boats on the water and a man dressed in a navy and white tracksuit, holding a stopwatch, was timing them from the bank and shouting instructions and encouragement. Lilly saw the school bus parked near to the water and assumed this was the PE teacher.

She walked over with Bonnie, who greeted the teacher by name.

"Hi, Mark."

He held up a hand, then as the winning boat reached the shore, stopped the watch and nodded.

"Sorry, Bonnie, had to get that time down. So, how are you?"

"I'm fine, thanks. Listen, I need to talk to one of your students, Quintin, for a moment if you can spare him?"

"Is it official, Bonnie?"

Bonnie shook her head. "Not at the moment. I'm just following up some loose ends pertaining to Edgar Stapleton's death. But, if it turns out to be more, I'll be in touch with his parents."

Mark nodded. "All right, but I'll be around if he needs me." He waved to two of the boys who were dragging a boat up onto the bank and Lilly saw it was Peter who had been teamed with Quintin. They both came jogging up.

"Quintin, Detective Phillips would like a quick word with you."

"What do you want with him?" Peter was quick to ask Bonnie.

"It's okay," Quintin said. He eyed Lilly thoughtfully. "I'll go with you."

"There's no need to come to the station," Bonnie said. "We can talk here."

Quintin shook his head. "No, it's okay, I'll come. I don't mind."

"Quintin, what's going on?" Peter said, but his friend ignored him.

Lilly and Bonnie had both noticed something in Quintin's voice and the look he gave them. He had something to say but didn't want to do it in front of either his teacher or his friend.

"All right, but I'll need to call your parents, Quintin."

"Why?" he asked, a look of panic appearing in his eyes.

"Because talking to you at the station makes it official and I cannot question you without a responsible adult, one that you trust, being present. It's the law to ensure both your welfare and your understanding of what is being asked. But, you're not under arrest, Quintin. I just want to confirm a few things, that's all."

"Can I choose who comes with me?"

Bonnie nodded. "Yes, providing you trust them to look after your well being."

"Will you come with me?" Quintin asked Lilly.

"Quintin, what are you doing?" Peter asked. "You don't have to go with them, you don't have to say anything."

"It's all right, Peter. I know what I'm doing. I won't be long. Well?" He said to Lilly. "Will you?"

Lilly glanced at Bonnie, then nodded. "Yes, of course I'll come with you."

Chapter Thirteen

LILLY HAD BEEN really taken aback when Quintin had requested her to accompany him. Of course, she couldn't say so to Bonnie on the drive back to Plumpton Mallet, as Quintin was in the back of the car. But as soon as they reached the station, and with a police constable taking the boy to an interview room, she pulled Bonnie to one side.

"Gosh, Bonnie, I'm so sorry. I had no idea Quintin would ask me to be present as his responsible adult."

Her friend chuckled. "Believe me, I know that. I could tell by the look of shock on your face."

"So, what's the plan, exactly?"

"I'm not making it official just yet. He obviously has something to tell us, so I'll let him talk. I can make a decision after that, depending on what he says."

"Okay."

"But the usual ground rules apply."

They found Quintin sitting quietly in the interview room with a PC standing against the wall. He gave a nod to Bonnie and left when she entered.

Bonnie started by asking the boy if he wanted anything to drink and when he declined, she put the letter on the table.

"Quintin, I realise you want to talk about something in particular, but first I want to ask you about this letter." She turned it to face him. "Did you write this and post it to The Agony Aunt cafe?"

He hesitated for a second, then nodded. "I didn't know what else to do." He was bordering on tears.

"It's all right, Quintin," Lilly said gently. "You did the right thing asking for help. Can you tell us what happened? From the beginning?"

Quintin began. He told them that when Peter and Oscar had decided to set up a rowing team, they asked Quintin if he wanted to be their fifth member? With Peter going out with Victoria and Alison being Victoria's best friend, they already had four. Quintin jumped at the chance. He loved all sports and played cricket in the summer and football during the season. But while he was enthusiastic, it didn't take long for him and the other team members to realise he didn't have the same stamina as the rest of him. Even the two girls could last longer than he could. And while they never said anything, at least not to his face, he could tell they were all becoming a bit frustrated with his lack of ability. There was no chance they would win any competitions with a weak member, and they were all having to work twice as hard to make up the slack. Quintin became upset and embarrassed about it, and rather than let the team down had told them, he would leave so they could replace him with someone better. But they were his friends and wouldn't hear of it.

One particular afternoon, after a really bad training session, Edgar Stapleton had taken him to one side and discussed additional one-on-one coaching to help build up his muscles and his strength. Quintin had agreed immediately. Training began the following week, three evenings at the gym and two extra afternoons on the water, but while he was gaining some strength and muscles, it wasn't enough and both of them were becoming discouraged. A few days later Edgar Stapleton offered him some tablets, performance enhancers, and assured him it was perfectly legal and safe, plenty of professional sportsman took them, and it would really help his performance.

"So, I took them. At first it was great, they really worked. The others couldn't believe how much better I was doing. My stamina improved, and I was gaining muscle. They thought it was down to all the extra training. But then I found I needed to take more in order to keep them working. I went to Mr Stapleton who told me that was normal and not to worry about it. But then I started to feel ill. Edgy and uneasy, and couldn't concentrate, like I had all this extra energy that I couldn't get rid of. Mr Stapleton suggested smoking a bit of pot to help me relax and take the edge off. I said no at first, but he told me it was legal for medical purposes. He said he knew someone I could go to, so I agreed. I got it, but I didn't want to do it on my own. I was a bit scared. So, I waited until Peter's birthday party and told Mr Stapleton that I'd got some."

"And what did he say?" Bonnie asked.

Quintin looked down at his lap. "He said we should try it together. So we did, just before the food came out. I had a couple of drags but I didn't really like it so he smoked most of it, but when we got back to the table, he said he was starting to feel a bit weird and gave me my money back." Lilly nodded. This is obviously what she'd seen when serving them desserts. Quintin continued. "He said we'd find someone else who could get some better stuff. After I'd eaten, I went and flushed the rest of it down the toilet. I kept getting interrupted so had to wait awhile. I didn't want anyone to see what I was doing. But when I got back outside, I heard screaming and ran down to the beach. I saw Preston doing CPR on someone, and when I got closer, I saw it was Mr Stapleton." Quintin began to cry. "If I wasn't so weak, Mr Stapleton would still be alive."

"Quintin, don't you dare blame yourself for what happened," Bonnie said sternly. "Edgar Stapleton should never have given you any drugs at all. Including the anabolic steroids."

"But he said they were legal."

"They are class C drugs, Quintin, which means while they are not illegal, they can only be sold by pharmacists and only with a prescription from a doctor. However, it is illegal to possess, import or export anabolic steroids if it's believed you're supplying or selling them. This includes giving them to friends. It also includes the pot. I'm sorry, Quintin, but Edgar Stapleton lied to you and he broke the law."

"Am I under arrest?"

"No, Quintin, I'm not going to arrest you, but consider this a final warning. It's your first offence, but it is a serious one. If you'd been in trouble before, whether a minor offence or not, then I would be referring you to the Youth Offending Team. However, you need to be aware that this will go on your police record. This is not the same as having a criminal record. I want you to understand that. It's for our records in case you get into trouble again in the future."

"I won't! I promise."

Bonnie nodded. "I hope not, Quintin, because two warnings are all you're allowed. Now, do you understand everything I have told you?"

"Yes. What happens now?"

A knock at the door and the entrance of a constable prevented Bonnie from answering.

"Sorry, Gov, we've got trouble in reception."

Lilly and Bonnie could hear shouting.

"Quintin, you can go home. But I would suggest you tell your parents what has happened as soon as you can. It will be better if they hear it from you first. All right? I do want you to understand I don't blame you for what happened with the drugs. You are young and impressionable, and as far as I'm concerned, were led astray by an adult you trusted."

Quintin nodded.

"One other thing. I suggest you look up the potential side-effects of continued anabolic steroid use. They are incredibly dangerous, particularly in someone as young as you are. Promise me you will never take them again?"

Quintin nodded. "I promise. I wasn't going to, anyway."

"All right. Good. Now, I'd better go and see what all the noise is about."

The three of them left the room and returned to the reception area where Lilly's heart sank as she realised who it was.

"I DON'T CARE WHAT she thinks," Susanna Stapleton shouted at the constable behind the reception counter. "She cannot bring one of Peter's friends in for questioning without an adult present."

"Is there a problem here?" Bonnie asked, as she, Lilly and Quintin entered.

Susanna spun round, a look of absolute fury on her face.

"Yes, there is. You're questioning a child without his parent's knowledge and without a responsible adult present. Have you at least provided a solicitor for him?"

"Perhaps you'd like to continue this conversation in private, Mrs Stapleton?"

"Absolutely not. I have no intention of speaking with you about anything in private. You'll just twist my words."

Bonnie shrugged. "All right, have it your way. Yes, Quintin is here as you can see, but he came voluntarily. In fact, he insisted, I was quite happy to talk to him at the rowing club. And as for having an adult present, he chose Miss Tweed himself. Isn't that right, Quintin?"

"Yes, it really is, Mrs Stapleton."

"Don't be a fool, Quintin. Don't you realise Detective Phillips and Lilly Tweed are as thick as thieves?"

"And he didn't need a solicitor," Bonnie continued, ignoring the jibe. "Because he was here purely to give some information that might help advance the investigation into the death of your husband. He is not under arrest, nor has he been charged with anything. However, as a result of what I have learned, I do have some questions for you, Mrs Stapleton."

"I have nothing to hide."

"I'll give you one more chance to discuss this in a private interview room rather than here, in reception."

"I've already said no."

"Mum," Peter said, but Susanna brushed him off.

Lilly stood close to Quintin. The two of them watched, wondering how Susanna would react when Bonnie asked the questions they knew were coming.

"Can you tell me why your husband would both encourage and supply class C drugs to a child who was purportedly under his care? Anabolic steroids and marijuana, to be precise."

Susanna looked as though someone had slapped her and Peter gasped audibly.

"What are you talking about? Do you realise who my husband was? He was an Olympic swimmer. One of the best in his field. He has the medals to prove it. He had no need for drugs! This is slander!"

"The post-mortem found both in his system, Susanna," Bonnie replied calmly.

"No. I don't believe you. It must be a mistake. Edgar would never knowingly take drugs."

"I'm afraid the evidence so far suggests otherwise."

"What evidence? You've got nothing except the word of child, who you should never have been speaking to in the first place. And a report from the post-mortem which must be a mistake, or more likely Edgar was fooled into believing what he took was something else. Something innocent. How dare you accuse my husband of giving drugs to children! You're not fit to be a police officer and I'll be demanding your resignation."

Susanna took a step forward, about to swing her handbag at Bonnie, but Peter grabbed her arm and pointed to the doorway. All eyes turned. Standing there were Preston and Lady Defoe.

Chapter Fourteen

THEY'D ARRIVED JUST in time to witness Susanna's entire outburst and, looking at the expression on Lady Defoe's face, Lilly could tell she found it distasteful and shocking in the extreme. But there was also a tinge of underlying sympathy, which Lilly found interesting. Having witnesses had taken the wind out of Susanna's sails and she moved back to stand next to her son and was finally quiet.

Everything was still for a second before the reception phone rang. The noise broke the spell and Bonnie turned to the new arrivals.

"Can I help you, Lady Defoe?"

"As a matter of fact, I think I may be able to help you, Detective Phillips. Preston and I were on our way to speak with the solicitor regarding Edgar's will when I saw Susanna's car parked outside. I thought perhaps she and I could talk in person prior to the meeting. However, having just witnessed her declarations about Edgar, I feel I need to share with you some information which I believe is pertinent to your case."

"Would you like to come through to my office?" Bonnie said.

Lady Defoe turned to Susanna. "I think you should hear what I have to say."

Susanna jutted out her chin, stubbornly.

"Peter and me are staying here."

Lady Defoe nodded. "Very well. Then I'll also remain here and explain, Detective Phillips."

Bonnie took out her notebook and pen while Lilly, Quintin and Preston took seats on the benches. Lady Defoe hesitated, then she too sat down.

"The general belief from those in the know, and believe me, there are not many, was that Edgar sent Preston away to boarding school when he was so young because of the circumstances of his birth, and also due to increased work commitments. Now, while that was partially the truth, it was not the whole story. My mother and father initially wanted nothing to do with either Preston or Edgar, but with the death of my sister, they mellowed a little. They had no intention of forming any sort of relationship with their grandson, but by the same token, they wanted to ensure he had a good upbringing and, in their own way, they intended to keep an eye on his welfare." She took a deep breath and sighed deeply. "Which they did. Unfortunately, they found out some information which infuriated, shocked and saddened them. It was at their insistence that Preston was sent away to school because they realised he was at risk." She paused, glancing at the sea of enrapt faces surrounding her. "The main reason Preston had to leave was due to his father's constant and increasing drug use. Edgar Stapleton was an addict."

"That's a lie!" Susanna shouted. "My husband has never had a drug problem. Not then and not now."

Peter rested his hand on her arm.

"Please, mum. I think we should listen to what Lady Defoe has to say."

"Thank you, Peter. I know it's difficult to hear, Susanna, but Edgar was always highly competitive, whether it be in sports or business, or whatever else he set his mind to. He was determined to be the best. When he started swimming, he was already very good, but it wasn't enough for him. He wanted to be an Olympian. Nothing else would do. That's when he began experimenting with performance enhancers. It was a slippery slope from then on, as you can imagine."

"You're saying he was using performance enhancers when he won his Olympic medals?" Bonnie asked. "I thought they tested for drug use?"

"They did, but the testing was relatively new and more advanced drugs were coming out all the time. In fact, many of those tested who had had negative results admitted years later in interviews they had actually taken the drugs. So it certainly wasn't a fool proof system. That being said, Edgar was exceptionally lucky not to have been caught. If he had stayed in competitive swimming, then he most certainly would have been. He was intelligent enough to realise this. Once he'd won his medals, which he considered the pinnacle of his career, he chose to retire and devote his spare time to training and coaching. Particularly his younger son's rowing team."

"Peter," Bonnie said, turning to the stunned boy. "Were you aware your dad was giving your teammates drugs?"

"No, I wasn't." Lilly believed him. He was well and truly shell-shocked.

"Lady Defoe, do you believe Edgar was still using drugs as recently as the party?"

"I'm afraid that's exactly what I'm saying. Edgar was a good father in many ways, but terrible in others. There's no two ways about it, Detective Phillips. He was, quite simply, a drug addict."

Susanna began to weep, and Peter put his arm around her shoulders. Quintin moved over to Bonnie and said something quietly, which the others didn't hear. Bonnie nodded and cleared her throat.

"If you'd like to remain here, you can. Otherwise, you're all free to go." No one moved. "All right. I'll be back shortly. Lilly, can I have a brief word?"

Lilly followed her through the door to the corridor, away from the others.

"What is it?"

"Quintin wants to give a formal statement. I'm taking him back through to my office. Can you keep an eye on things here? Listen to what's said and tell me if you hear anything I need to know? I'll also have a constable in place, just in case things get heated."

Lilly nodded. "Of course, but who will be with Quintin?"

"I've asked my Sergeant to call the duty solicitor, she's on her way. And he's also in the process of tracking down his parents."

"Is Quintin aware of all that?" Bonnie nodded. "All right. I'll see you shortly."

Lilly returned to the reception area and found Lady Defoe had moved to sit next to Susanna, and Preston was with his younger brother. She sat nearby, not wanting to intrude, but she was close enough to listen should anything new come to light that she could pass onto Bonnie.

WHILE THEY WERE waiting for Quintin and Bonnie to return, Lilly wondered if Lady Defoe would bring up the subject of Preston's inheritance. Consequently, she was on edge, ready to spring into action. Who knew what Susanna's reaction would be? But Susanna was busy texting on her phone and Lady Defoe was sitting regally at her side, remaining quiet and patient. The boys were talking quietly.

"You didn't know?" Preston asked Peter. "Quintin never said anything to you?"

"Nothing. He was training and working out a lot. I just thought it was down to that."

"And you didn't notice any change in his behaviour?"

Peter shrugged. "He was a bit hyper sometimes, but I thought it was the excitement and nervousness of the competitions we had coming up. We stood a really good chance of winning some decent races and getting medals this year and he would be part of the championship team. We were all pumped about it."

"What about dad?"

"Preston, I swear I had no idea he was taking drugs. Don't you think I would have said something if I had?"

"Sorry. Yeah, I know you would."

"Did you know? About dad, I mean?" Peter asked his older brother.

Preston shook his head. "I had absolutely no idea until my aunt told me yesterday. Makes sense of a lot of things about my life, though."

Taking a written statement from Quintin didn't take as long as Lilly had expected. But, she supposed, he'd already given the information once. Forty-five minutes later, Bonnie escorted him back into the reception area.

"Thank you for waiting, everyone. There's no need to stay any longer. I'm just waiting for Quintin's parents to pick him up."

"I've just been messaging them," Susanna said. "They're on their way, but will be awhile. They asked me to take him home with me and they'll pick him up from there. Are you ready to go, Quintin?"

Bonnie gave Susanna a curt nod and turned to Quintin. "Are you happy with that arrangement, Quintin, or do you want to wait and have your parents pick you up here?"

Susanna huffed at having her benevolence questioned, but thankfully, she didn't start an argument.

"No, it's fine. I'll go with them."

"Preston," Susanna said. "I owe you an apology. I wish I'd known before about Edgar's drug problem and the reason you were sent away to school. Would you like to join us?"

You could have heard a pin drop in the police station waiting room.

"Um, yes, okay. Thanks," Preston said, looking at his aunt.

"Thank you, Susanna, that's very kind of you," Lady Defoe said. "I'll come along as well. There are some important things we need to discuss. I'm sure we can have a civilised conversation at your house."

Susanna hesitated for a second, then relented. "Yes, of course we can. It's time we cleared the air."

"I'll telephone the solicitor and rearrange our appointment."

Lilly could tell Peter was thrilled his mother was including Preston and Lady Defoe in the invitation. For the first time since his father had died, Lilly could see a spark of hope in the boy's face.

She and Bonnie stood side-by-side, watching as the unlikely group left the station. Peter telling Quintin and Preston about a new video game he'd recently bought, and the two women following with indulgent smiles on their faces.

"WELL, I CERTAINLY didn't expect that," Bonnie said.

"Maybe it will all work out," Lilly said. "So, what happened with Quintin?"

"Come through to my office. I need a coffee. Do you want one?"

"Crikey, no thanks. It's like having a cup of molasses. I don't know how you can drink it."

Having made herself a large mug of strong black coffee and gulped half of it down with an appreciative sigh, Bonnie told Lilly what additional information Quintin had given her.

"I obviously needed to confirm unequivocally he had nothing to do with Edgar's death, and he remembered that even though he'd tried to be careful, he'd actually been seen in the toilets getting rid of the pot by a boy he knows from school. I rang the school and spoke to the witness. He corroborates Quintin's story. Almost immediately after that, the call went out from the beach that Edgar had been found. Quintin was in the company of a lot of other people prior to the incident so is alibied the entire time, apart from when he was alone with Edgar trying the pot. But we know Edgar was alive for a while after that. Quintin did not murder Edgar."

"I didn't think for a minute he had. But it begs the question, who did?" Lilly said.

"It does. And quite frankly, I'm no nearer finding out who it was."

"Bonnie, I'm starving. Do you want to go to the cafe and get something to eat?"

"Good idea."

"I'll meet you there. I just need to go to the shop and check Stacey is all right."

"No problem, I'll meet you at the cafe."

Lilly left the station and jogged down the road. Turning right onto the market square, she continued across and entered the Tea Emporium where she found Stacey putting away some tea sets.

"Hey! You've been gone ages. Is everything OK?"

"I'm so sorry, Stacey. We ended up at the police station."

She grabbed a cup of rooibos and cinnamon tea, then sat at the counter, adjusting her position so Earl could sit and knead on her knee, and brought Stacey up to date with everything that had happened since she'd left with Bonnie that morning.

"Wow. So they all just left together like happy families?" Stacey said.

Lilly laughed. "Well, the three boys certainly did. I'm not sure about Susanna and Lady Defoe yet. It was a bit strained. Time will tell."

"I can't believe Edgar was a drug addict, and he gave them to poor Quintin. But I'm glad he told the truth. Those things are really dangerous long-term, especially when you're still young like Quintin is."

"I know. I was googling the side effects and dangers of anabolic steroids when I was with Bonnie. It's really frightening. I don't think Quintin had any idea how unsafe they are."

"That's because he was given them by an adult he trusted and admired. Why would he question it?"

"You're absolutely right about that. The good news is he won't be doing it again. I think he's really scared about everything that's happened and Bonnie has informed him of some of the side effects and told him to look the rest up himself. If that doesn't put him off drugs for life, I don't know what will. Anyway, I need to go to the cafe now to meet Bonnie. Have you had anything to eat?"

"Yes, I have. Fred popped in with something. You go, I'll be fine here. But I want all the details when I see you tomorrow."

"I'll tell you as much as I'm able," Lilly promised.

The cafe was busy but not full when she arrived. Abigail had gone off on some errands, but Frederick was in his usual spot behind the Barista station. He worked almost as many hours as Stacey did, and Lilly wondered when they had time to go out and be a couple together. But it seemed to suit them. She gave him a quick wave and joined Bonnie at the back of the cafe. She'd wangled one of the comfy banquettes, partially obscured by a giant potted fern. Perfect for a private conversation.

"Do you know who supplied Quintin with the marijuana, Bonnie?"

"He doesn't know. It was a number to text, then a drop off point where he had to leave the money. They were obviously watching him because he got another text immediately after that, telling him where he could pick up the pot. He never saw anyone, and he went the next day to see if his money had been picked up. It had. The phone was obviously a burner, as it's no longer active. We're keeping an eye on the drop point, but I doubt they'll use it again. Whoever it was is very savvy. It's a growing problem."

"I had no idea. It's hard to imagine somewhere as peaceful and beautiful as Plumpton Mallet having a drug problem."

Bonnie nodded. "You'd better believe it, Lilly. Particularly among the youth."

"So, what about suspects? Have you anybody in mind?"

"Not at the moment."

A waitress appeared and took their food order, returning a moment later with a chamomile tea for Lilly and yet another strong black coffee for Bonnie. After she'd moved to serve another table, Bonnie continued.

"I'm really stuck with this one, Lilly. I don't think it was the drugs that killed Edgar. It was the fact he was held under water until he drowned. That's my belief. All the drugs did was make him unable to fight back."

"Is that in the post-mortem report?"

"I'm due to go over there next. They should have finished the full report by now."

"Want a second set of eyes?"

Bonnie laughed. "Honestly, Lilly, I don't know why you bother asking. You'll tag along whether I want you to or not."

"True."

They had both chosen one of Abigail's new pasta dishes and Bonnie was impressed.

"This is great. Do you do take-outs?"

"Of course. There's a deliver service as well within three miles of the town centre."

"Excellent. I'll be having my food delivered to the station from now on. Remind me to pick up a menu on the way out."

Chapter Fifteen

ONCE THEY'D LEFT the cafe, the two women walked up to the police station to collect Bonnie's car. As they left Plumpton Mallet, taking the main road to the hospital, Bonnie turned to her friend.

"Do you mind if I talk through what we know so far? It helps to bounce ideas around, and quite frankly, I could do with all the help I can get at the moment."

"You say the same thing every time, Bonnie," Lilly said. "But you always end up solving the case. Where do you want to start?"

"The beginning. At Peter's birthday party. I arrived after the fact, but you were there from the beginning. Tell me again what happened."

"I remember hearing the shout from the beach and a crowd of people surrounding Edgar while Preston gave him CPR. I hurried over and moved people out of the way. Victoria was there, which surprised me because I thought she'd left after the altercation with Peter. Actually, I saw Victoria in the car-park before that. She stole a crate of my tea."

"What? Why didn't you tell me? You didn't report it?"

Lilly shook her head. "No, I didn't because I wanted to see if she'd confess to the theft, and she did. I've got it back with no harm done. It's not relevant to the case, Bonnie."

"I'll be the judge of that. Carry on."

"Oscar and Alison were both there when Edgar was pulled from the water. Various guests called the ambulance. Abigail called you. But by the time the paramedics got there, it was too late. Preston had stopped trying to get his heart beating again. It was obvious to everyone who witnessed his attempt that Edgar was long gone."

"Do you remember anyone at all acting out of character or suspicious in any way, Lilly? No matter how small?"

"Not then, but I did afterwards. While they were all having dessert, I saw Edgar secretly pass a wad of money to Quintin. With the shock of Edgar's death, I didn't remember until later. It fits what Quintin told us."

"Did anyone else see that?"

"Oscar was sitting on Edgar's other side. If he saw what happened, he didn't say anything. He was talking to Edgar about the team's chances, and Edgar said they would definitely win this season."

Bonnie indicated, drove round the round-about and took the third left onto the hospital road before replying.

"How could he be so certain they'd win? Did he mention that?"

"No, but I thought it could be because of the girls on the team. I found out it was probably Edgar who was behind Victoria's decision to leave."

"In what way?"

"Peter asked her to leave and then broke up with her. Basically, the boys, with quite a lot of encouragement from Edgar, who seemed to want an all-boy team, made it difficult for her to stay. It was a distressing time for her, especially as Alison initially sided with the boys. She felt like she'd lost everything."

"Do you think she was angry enough to kill Edgar?"

Lilly stared out of the window, watching the houses go past as Bonnie changed gear to drive down the hill, thinking about the answer.

"Initially, I would have said yes, but now, I really don't think so."

"She's on my list of suspects, Lilly."

"Bonnie, we're talking about a child here."

"I know, and as much as it leaves a sour taste in my mouth, it's happened before. Juvenile centres and prisons are full of youngsters who've committed heinous crimes. It's horrifying, but a sad state in today's world. If Victoria felt she'd lost everything because of Edgar, then she has a motive, Lilly. I can't rule her out."

"No, all right, I understand. So, who else is on your radar?"

"Preston."

"Preston? But he helped pull Edgar out of the water and tried to save his life. You weren't there, Bonnie. You have no idea how valiantly that boy fought to save his father. It was heartbreaking to watch."

"I hate to say it, Lilly, but it could all have been an act. It wouldn't be the first time for that scenario, either. In Preston's case, he was shipped off to boarding school when he was still in short trousers. Hardly any contact with his father or extended family. Let's face it, he was pretty much abandoned. He was born out of wedlock and his mother died not a year after he was born. Edgar married another woman who obviously disliked him and had another son who he doted on. You're not telling me Preston harboured no resentment at all?"

Lilly shook her head. "I don't know how you do this job, Bonnie. You have to take such a cynical outlook on life. Automatically seeing the worst in people before you can see the good. Doesn't it wear you out?"

"Of course it does, but it's not everyone, Lilly. And actually I'm a bit offended by the fact you think I can't see the good in most people. Of course I can. But it's my job. I'd never catch anyone if I thought they were all angels."

"I'm sorry, Bonnie. I don't mean to hurt you, you know that. I admire you hugely for being able to do this job and not go completely crazy. Forgive me?"

Bonnie nodded. "Of course I forgive you."

"You're right about, Preston. He admitted he and Edgar weren't close, but I can't see him as a murderer. He was stunned when I told him he was the sole beneficiary of his father's will. He had absolutely no idea."

"Wait, a minute. It was you who told him?"

"It wasn't intentional. It kind of came up in conversation, and in my defense I honestly thought he already knew. Susanna was spitting feathers in my shop when she found out. Had a tantrum about it, actually. Archie witnessed it too. I felt sure she was on her way to have it out with Preston when she left."

"Whether he knew about the money or not, he is still a main suspect."

"I'm not disagreeing with you, but you should have seen him at the party. He was exhausted both physically and emotionally after trying to save Edgar."

"Or was he exhausted from holding a fully grown man under the water until he died?"

Lilly looked bleakly at her friend as she pulled into the hospital car-park and found a space near the door. Turning off the engine and pulling on the handbrake, Bonnie sat back and looked at Lilly.

"So, talking of Archie, how is that going?"

Lilly couldn't help but grin.

"You're glowing, Miss Tweed."

Lilly nodded. "It's going very well. I can't believe it's taken so long."

"You and half of Plumpton Mallet."

"I'm sure Archie feels the same."

Bonnie scoffed. "Of course he does. The man has been walking six inches above the pavement ever since you got together. I'm really thrilled for you both, Lilly. I mean that. You both deserve a lot of happiness and there's nothing I like better than watching two of my closest friends finally realise they belong together. And on that sappy note, let's go and see what Doctor Perry has for us."

LILLY HAD ONLY been to the mortuary once before, when one of the guests at a wedding reception she was catering had been found dead. Bonnie flashed her badge at the receptionist, who waved her through with a nod and a smile, and they began the descent down three flights of stairs to the basement.

At the bottom they pushed through the double doors, which had had a new coat of paint since the last time Lilly had visited, but still in the horrible shade of dull green that she associated with municipality buildings everywhere, and walked to the end of the corridor where the office was located. Bonnie knocked on the open door and the man inside looked up.

"Detective Phillips, and, Miss Tweed," Doctor Perry said, standing and inviting them to take a seat. "Come for my report on the Stapleton death, I assume."

Bonnie nodded. "Have you found anything new?"

"I was just about to phone you. There is something else since we last spoke."

Bonnie sat up, alert. "What is it?"

"Initially, I thought it was paint," Doctor Perry said, reaching for a manilla folder on the top of a teetering pile at the edge of his desk. Lilly felt a bit queasy when she realised all of those files represented a deceased person.

"Paint?" Bonnie said, frowning, while Lilly's heart skipped a beat as an overheard conversation swum to the front of her mind.

Doctor Perry nodded. "Tiny flecks on the back of the victim's neck, embedded in the bruise we found where he was forcibly held under the water. Cause of death is officially drowning, by the way. But, I was wrong about the paint. Well, not wrong, per se. Partially incorrect. Here," he said, handing over the post-mortem report. "See for yourself."

Bonnie almost snatched the file from Doctor Perry's grasp and flipped through to the findings page, with Lilly leaning over her shoulder to read the document at the same time.

"Well, this certainly changes things," Bonnie said.

Lilly, who was a bit slower to read, suddenly gasped and grabbed Bonnie's arm.

"Oh, my god, Bonnie, I know who it is!"

Chapter Sixteen

AFTER THANKING DOCTOR Perry profusely for the information, Bonnie rushed from the room with Lilly chasing after her. She'd just explained to the detective what she'd remembered; the seemingly innocuous conversation that had happened while they were setting up for Peter's party.

They took the stairs to the ground floor two at a time, Lilly gasping as she charged through the door into the main reception area of the hospital. Bonnie was already in the car-park.

"Bonnie, will you please wait for me?"

"Come on, hurry up."

"I don't understand why you're in such a rush. They aren't going anywhere. They don't even know we've worked it out."

"Because it's possible there'll be another murder, Lilly, and I'm trying to stop it. Get in the car."

Lilly jumped in the passenger seat and slammed the door, yanking the seatbelt and trying to get it fastened while Bonnie careened out of the site and onto the main road. Taking a left turn up the hill rather than the returning in the same direction they'd arrived.

"What do you mean?"

"Think about it! That little scene in the police station was all for show. Happy families, my eye. I should have seen the undercurrent of resentment."

"Oh, Bonnie! I'm such an idiot." Lilly said as she realised what her friend meant. "I should have seen it, too. Quickly! Can't you go any faster?"

"Not without putting us and everyone else on the road in danger!" Bonnie snapped, stress and anxiety rising to the surface.

Lilly decided to stay quiet. Bonnie needed to concentrate. The last thing they needed was to be involved in an accident.

Bonnie drove fast but totally in control, electing to take the moor road on the opposite side of the river to Plumpton Mallet town. There was less traffic on this winding country road and the house they were going to was situated on the far side, up the hill at the top of the woodland the town was famous for. It was a wealthy neighbourhood, filled with large detached homes in half and full acre grounds.

Under normal circumstances it would take twenty minutes, the speed Bonnie was driving it would probably take half the time, but even that seemed interminably long to Lilly considering the urgency and what could be at stake.

Bonnie took a short-cut left before the hill that dropped down to the riverside, then a right, slowly driving over a cattle grid and a humped back bridge just wide enough for one car, and wound through farmland on a semi-rural track before joining the proper road once more. Three minutes later they reached the edge of the houses and she turned right, driving a few metres down the hill and parking outside a tall, black, wrought-iron gate set in the middle of an eight foot yew hedge.

"I don't want anyone to get suspicious, Lilly," Bonnie said, getting out of the car. "We'll go in as though we know nothing and are here with just a couple of follow-up questions. I do not want anything to tip them off."

Lilly nodded. "Of course."

Bonnie got out her phone and hit speed dial. "I'm just going to let the station know where we are."

The call made and with her team on standby, Bonnie pushed opened the gate and strode up the path. She lifted the yacht shaped brass door knocker and rapped three times. The door was answered a few seconds later.

"OH, HI."

"Hello, Peter," Bonnie said. "Can we come in?"

"Yes. Did you want mum?"

"Is she here?"

"She's in dad's office."

"Is Preston still here?"

"He's with her. They're going through some of dad's stuff. Preston was interested."

"Was he?" Bonnie said, shooting a glance at Lilly. "Is Lady Defoe still here, Peter?"

"In the sitting room. I was showing her the photograph albums. Is something wrong?"

"No, don't worry. I've just got a couple more questions, that's all. Where is your dad's office?"

"Outside, at the end of the garden. Mum wasn't happy about clients coming into the house all the time, so he had it built down there. Shall I show you?"

"Don't worry, I'm sure we can find it," Bonnie said, striding down the hall. "Best not to leave Lady Defoe on her own, Peter," she finished with a smile, hoping to put him at ease.

"Is Quintin still here?" Lilly asked.

Peter shook his head. "No, his mum and dad came for him about an hour ago."

"Okay, thank you, Peter. We'll leave you to your family albums. We won't be long."

Peter nodded and returned to the living room.

Once he'd disappeared, Lilly and Bonnie picked up the pace and ended up in a large open-plan kitchen and dining room, where they found the back door. It opened up onto an expansive flagged patio area with a comfortable seating area, outdoor dining set and two wooden gazebos. A two foot high wall planted with spring flowers flanked a set of stone steps that dropped to a verdant lawn. Bonnie and Lilly charged down them two at a time and ran across the lawn, dodging large evergreens and bushes as they went. Beyond a six foot high privet hedge they came to a modern chrome and glass building, with an empty car-port to one side and a gate in the fence leading to the road behind. Bonnie looked back.

"You can't even see the house from here."

She approached the building and tried the door. It opened, but with the whole front wall being an expanse of glass, it was apparent there was no one inside. But what they did discover was a mess.

"There's been a struggle in here, Lilly," Bonnie said, taking in the chaotic scene.

She moved to the only door in the single open-plan room and opened it. As she'd expected, it was the bathroom, but it was empty.

"Bonnie, over here," Lilly called out.

Bonnie dashed over and found Lilly crouched behind the large desk.

"There's blood on the carpet here, and on the corner of the desk. Oh, Bonnie, are we too late?"

Bonnie didn't answer. Pulling her phone from her pocket, she started barking out orders to her team. Lilly waited until she'd finished.

"What now?"

"The car is missing from the car-port and there is direct access from the road behind. They could have left at anytime. Do you know what sort of car either Susanna or Edgar own?"

"Susanna has a dark blue sporty golf. I don't know what Edgar drove."

"Well, I saw the golf parked at the front. Come on, we need to get back to the house and ask Peter how long they've been gone. I don't suppose you've any idea where they would have gone?" Bonnie asked her as they ran back up the lawn.

"I've no idea. They could be anywhere. Peter might know."

Half way up the lawn, they met Lady Defoe coming down.

"Is everything all right? Peter said you'd arrived."

"Preston and Susanna are missing. Do you know when they went down to the office?"

"Missing? Gosh, it must have been about twenty minutes ago, I think."

They were moving back up to the house, and Peter was waiting for them in the kitchen.

"What's going on?"

"Your mother and brother are not in the office, Peter," Lady Defoe said.

"What do you mean?"

"Peter, what car did your father drive?"

"A silver BMW. It's parked in the car-port."

Bonnie shook her head. "Not any more. Do you know the registration?" Peter reeled it off, and Bonnie phoned the station telling them to be on the look out for it and to call her immediately when it was spotted, then turned back to Peter. "Do you have any idea where they might have gone?"

"I... I don't know," the boy stammered, confused. "I didn't know they had gone. What's happening? Why would mum and Preston go off in dad's car? What is it you're not telling me?"

"I'm sorry, Peter, but I can't share that with you at the moment, but we've found signs of a struggle and a small amount of blood in the office. It's now a crime-scene so no one can go down there, do you understand? I have a team on the way."

"Blood? Crime scene?" Peter repeated numbly.

"We need to find them, Peter. Can you think of anything either of them said before they went to your father's office?"

Peter shook his head. "No, nothing. Mum just mentioned a few of dad's trophies and photos were down there if Preston wanted to have a look. But what does that have to do with anything? Why would they leave? Wait! Mum will have her phone on her. Dad installed the 'find my phone' app on all of them. We can find out that way."

"Good boy," Lady Defoe said, as Peter started swiping his own phone. When he'd found what he was looking for, he handed it to Bonnie. There was a map and a red pin with the designation 'mum' on the listed phone.

"Of course!" Bonnie said, returning Peter's phone. "They're on their way to the rowing club. Come on, Lilly, we don't have a moment to lose. Lady Defoe, please stay here and look after Peter. My team is on the way and I'll keep you both updated as soon as I know more."

Lady Defoe nodded and put her arm around Peter's shoulder. "Of course. And detective, please be careful."

IN THE CAR, Bonnie quickly radioed the station and asked for an ambulance to get to the rowing club as quickly as possible. "I'm on my way, but I don't know what we'll find. God forbid we're too late. And I want two PCs over there asap."

With everything confirmed, Bonnie put her foot down and raced down the hill to the main road. Turning left then right at the end of the field next to the river, she drove over the new bridge, then turned right again along the main road which, a couple of minutes later, turned into open countryside on the outskirts of Plumpton Mallet.

"I feel like we've come full circle, Bonnie," Lilly said, clutching her seat as the detective put her foot down to race up the hill. "This all started at the rowing club. Now it looks like it's going to end there."

Bonnie shifted gears and shook her head. "This started long before then. The rowing club is just where we got involved. As far as I can tell, the Stapletons are the epitome of a dysfunctional family, Lilly, and there's a huge amount that's happened in the past that we're not aware of."

"Enough for another murder?"

Bonnie nodded. "It's certainly looking that way."

Twenty minutes later, they shot into the rowing club car-park and stopped with a spray of gravel. Followed by a panda car, which came to a halt next to them. Bonnie jumped out.

"Right, you're with me," she said, pointing to a young constable. "Lilly, Davidson, you two go down the lake path. We'll check the club house. Davidson, use your whistle immediately if you see either of them."

"Yes, Gov," Davidson said, and pelted off down the footpath with Lilly racing after him, trying, but failing, to keep up with him.

She was halfway down the dirt foot path when her boot slipped from under her and she slid down the bank. Frantically scrabbling and snatching tufts of grass and exposed tree roots to prevent falling into the water. She desperately called out to the police officer, but there was no answer. Then she heard the shrill whistle. Three times it sounded. Urgent and desperate. He'd found something!

With renewed strength borne of adrenaline laced with fear, she heaved herself up the bank, oblivious to the bleeding cuts on her hands and face from the brambles. She reached the path on hands and knees, staggered upright and limped down the path as fast as she could. Heart beating wildly, shivering with cold sweat and dreading what she'd find.

It was the worst thing she could think of.

"Oh, no!" she shouted, barrelling down onto the man-made, stony beach.

Davidson was pulling a lifeless body from the water up onto the stones, while trying to fend off an attack from behind. Lilly raced to his side, fell to her knees, and frantically began CPR.

"Come on! Breath!" she yelled, counting the chest compressions, then giving two rescue breaths, followed by more chest compressions. "Please. Come on!" she begged, oblivious to the ruckus behind her.

Suddenly there was a heave and a cough and Preston Stapleton rolled onto his side vomiting up lake water. She felt hands on her shoulders, pulling her away as the paramedics took over. It was Bonnie. Lilly burst into tears.

"It's all right, Lilly," Bonnie said. "You saved him. He's going to be fine. Lilly, can you hear me? He's alive. Preston is alive."

Lilly nodded.

"Come on, you need to get those cuts seen to."

Lilly allowed herself to be guided up to the path by Bonnie. She was in a daze, emotionally and physically drained.

"I'm all right, Bonnie, honestly. It looks worse than it is. I just got a bit scratched up when I fell down the bank."

"You're limping."

"I twisted my knee slightly. It's fine. I'll clean up in the club house. So, where's Susanna?"

"On her way to the station. Formally under arrest for the murder of Edgar and the attempted murder of Preston. He'll need to be taken to hospital, but it looks like he'll be fine, thanks to you."

"I take it you'll be interviewing Susanna when you get back?"

"I will. Please don't ask to sit in, Lilly."

Lilly smiled. "I wouldn't dream of it. You'll let me know what she says, though?"

"Of course I will."

Chapter Seventeen

A COUPLE OF DAYS later, an hour before the shop was due to open, everyone met at The Tea Emporium, now the case had been solved. Lilly and Stacey had set up the table in the storeroom and made tea. Abigail had turned up with breakfast baps for everyone and Archie had brought his notebook. Bonnie arrived with all the details of her interviews with Susanna.

Once they were all settled, Lilly asked the question that had been burning in her mind ever since she and Archie had overheard the conversation between Susanna and her solicitor.

"I don't understand why Edgar would leave everything to Preston and exclude Peter and his wife. Did she explain, Bonnie?"

Bonnie wiped the tomato sauce from her fingertips before answering.

"She didn't know what had happened at the time, but I've since spoken with the solicitor. Edgar dealt with the senior partner of the old law firm years ago when Preston was young. Naturally, being unmarried with no other heirs, he left everything to his son. But, when he married and he and Susanna had Peter, he obviously wrote a new one. This gave Susanna the house and contents and an income, enabling her to keep it. She didn't work, you see. The rest was split equally between the two boys. Again, he dealt with the senior partner, but he retired shortly afterwards to the Algarve and sold the firm to another practice. Incidentally, he died a couple of years ago. Time passed and I assume Edgar thought everything was in order. But it wasn't."

You could have heard a pin drop in the storeroom as all eyes were on Bonnie, everyone waiting for the revelation.

"Edgar Stapleton never signed the new will, thus rendering it invalid."

"Good Lord," Archie said, forgetting to make notes for a moment. He turned to Lilly. "Remind me to double check I've signed mine, will you?"

"But couldn't she have contested it?" Abigail said, pouring more tea.

"She could have tried, but having spoken to the solicitor, he doubted it would have been successful. Besides, she'd already killed Edgar before she knew about the will not being legal."

"So, she killed him for the money?" Stacey asked.

"Partly," Bonnie said.

"Was it also about the drugs?" Lilly asked.

Bonnie nodded and took her refilled cup from Abigail.

"Thanks. Yes, Lady Defoe was right, Edgar was an addict. Susanna broke down and eventually shared that Edgar had been both mentally and physically abusive towards her many times while under the influence. She knew then he was back on the drugs regularly and it would only be a matter of time before he lost his business, the money, and the house. She couldn't live with him anymore and she was dreading the day when he became physically abusive towards Peter. The drugs changed his personality and she just couldn't trust him anymore. She'd confronted him before, and it always ended the same way. She knew then the only way to save herself and her son, and keep a roof over their head, was for Edgar to die." Bonnie shrugged. "That's when she started putting her plan together."

"And Peter never noticed any of this?" Archie asked.

"Susanna was very careful to keep it all from him. And Edgar, for his part, made sure not to resort to violence in front of his son. Susanna said it was the main reason why he built the office. It was a place he escaped to away from his family."

"So, Susanna tried to kill Preston because she thought she and Peter would get everything after he'd died?" Stacey asked, frowning.

"That's what was going through her mind," Bonnie said. "But she admits by that time she wasn't thinking rationally. She was living in a state of anger and depression, although she hid it exceptionally well. Then again, she's had a lot of practice putting a brave face on things while her personal life was in tatters. Preston hasn't written a will, so if he died, then it would become a legal minefield and everyone would lose."

Archie was busily scratching notes, then posed a question.

"How is it a middle aged woman wrestled a strong young man half her age into the car in the first place?"

"She drugged him. Ironic isn't it?" Bonnie said. "She crushed several of the sedatives the doctor had prescribed her and put them in the tea she served. Once she could see they were beginning to take effect, she suggested a visit to his father's office to show him the trophies and stuff his father had won, but there were some things she and Peter would like to keep, she'd said to him. A lie, obviously. Now he was due to inherit it all she wanted to check he was happy about them having these things. I don't know if you've met him, Archie?" Archie shook his head. "Well, despite the way he looks, he's a really pleasant and polite young man. There was no way he would refuse. Especially because he genuinely thought Susanna was trying to make amends for the past by welcoming him into the family. You have to remember, a family was the one thing he'd never really had."

"But what about the blood we found in the office, Bonnie?" Lilly asked.

"Once he realised Susanna had drugged him, he tried to fight back. She said she had no choice but to punch him. The blood was from the resulting nose bleed. He was weak and dizzy at that point, and she had no problem getting him into the car. He was in and out of consciousness the whole journey to the rowing club. When they arrived, he was easy to manhandle down the foot path and into the water. Susanna is physically strong, plays tennis, works out at the gym. We got there just in time for Lilly to bring Preston back from the brink of death."

Archie leaned over and gave her a hug.

"Well done, Lilly."

There was a chorus of agreement from the others, and Lilly blushed furiously.

"How did you know it was Susanna?" Stacey asked the detective.

"That also was, Lilly," Bonnie said. "I'll let her tell you."

"It was the minute fragments of what Doctor Perry first thought was paint found on the back of Edgar's neck. Further tests revealed it was actually nail varnish in three distinct colours. Dark blue, light blue and white. The club colours. When we were setting up for the party, Preston mentioned how nice they looked and Susanna said she'd had them done, especially for the party. She was the only one who had. It couldn't have been anyone else."

A few minutes later, the group dispersed. It was almost opening time. As the others left the store room Archie hung back with Lilly.

"You had me worried there, Lilly. Look at your poor face and hands."

"Oh, Archie, it's just a few scratches. I've had much worse. They will heal in no time."

"And what about your knee?"

"It's fine. Stop worrying."

"I'm so proud of you, you know? You saved that boy's life with your quick thinking."

"I just happened to be there at the right time, Archie. Anyone would have done the same thing."

Archie shook his head.

"I don't agree, but I'm not going to argue with you. Instead, I'm going to take you out for dinner tonight. Your choice where we go. How about it?"

Lilly nodded.

"I'd love to, Archie."

Chapter Eighteen

IT WAS A bright, warm and sunny Sunday a few weeks later and Lilly, along with Archie, Stacey, Abigail and remarkably Bonnie, who had a rare day off, were at the rowing club watching the first races of the season. It hadn't taken Stacey long to join her college friends, and Bonnie had wandered off not long after her.

"I'm glad we're not catering this event," Abigail said, looking at the crowds in the two-tier, purpose-built stands surrounding the starting line at the edge of lake.

"You and me both," Lilly said. "If it wasn't for the fact Peter, Quintin, Victoria and Alison are racing as a team for the first time, I doubt I'd be here."

"They have done very well, haven't they?" Abigail said. "Considering all they've been through? I'm very glad Peter finally saw sense and got rid of Oscar."

Archie agreed. "They're working together as a cohesive team now. In fact, they're currently odds-on favourite to win."

"Have you been betting on the race, Archie?"

"Yes, Miss Tweed, I have. I put a fiver on for you too."

"Oh, I've just seen a friend of mine. Do you mind if I join her? She's on her own?"

"Of course not, Abigail," Lilly said. "It's our day off. You can do what you like."

Once Abigail had left, Lilly turned to Archie.

"How was the interview with Quintin's parents for your article?"

"Honestly? It was pretty tough, actually. They wanted to know my stance on the situation first, to make sure I wasn't going to write the boy up as a drug addict. I assured them that wasn't my intention. Quintin was taken advantage of by Edgar, a man who should never have been in a position of authority in the first place. And that was the angle I was taking. Once that was out of the way, they ran the gamut of emotions as you'd expect, but ultimately they are hugely proud of their son for coming forward when it mattered and were more than willing to talk. They don't want what happened to be repeated."

Lilly nodded. "I'm very glad about that, Archie. Quintin is such a good kid I'd hate for this incident to follow him around for the rest of his life."

"It won't. When the article comes out tomorrow, everyone will see what you do. A great kid who was wronged by his coach." Archie squeezed her hand. "Looks like we're about to get company."

Lilly glanced to where Archie was looking and saw Lady Defoe climbing the steps towards them.

"Lady Defoe, I didn't realise you were here."

"Hello, Lilly, Mr Brown. I'm down in the pavilion with my husband and Preston," she said, indicating the blue and white striped tent to the right of the stands. "We're sponsoring the event. Do you mind if I join you for a moment?"

"Please do."

"I was just going to get drinks," Archie said. "Can I get you anything?"

Lady Defoe shook her head.

"No, thank you, Mr Brown."

"Call me Archie, please. Lilly, the usual?"

"Yes, thanks, Archie."

"I owe you a great debt for saving the life of my nephew, Lilly," Lady Defoe said when they were alone. "I want you to know if there is anything I can do for you now or at anytime in the future, please ask. I mean it. If it wasn't for you, I would no longer have Preston, and he means a very great deal to me."

"How is he?"

"He's recovered health-wise, but is still having flashbacks in the form of nightmares, which is perfectly understandable. They will lessen in time. Apart from that, he's remarkable. He's really taking the part of 'big brother' seriously and is a tremendous help and much needed support for Peter."

"Are they still living in the house?"

Lady Defoe shook her head.

"No, I've given them one of the empty cottages on our land, although they both seem to prefer living at the main house with us. It's lovely to have young people in the house again. Edgar and Susanna's former home is now on the market and Preston is speaking with the solicitor about giving Peter half of the inheritance. Some will be put in trust for Peter's education should he decide to go on to university when he's finished his schooling. Or for whatever he needs it for, within reason. They are both being remarkably sensible about it. I'm incredibly relieved Peter has his brother to lean on now he's lost his parents."

"He's not in touch with Susanna?"

"At the moment, he wants nothing to do with her. That may change going forward, of course. I hope it does. My husband, I will support him no matter what he decides, but I think it's best for the moment that he concentrates on building his new life and his future. He's part of the Defoe family now."

They chatted for a few more minutes, then Lady Defoe got up to return to the sponsor's pavilion before the start of the first race.

"Oh, while I remember. The election for the new town mayor is this year and, as usual, there is to be a fundraiser at the Town Hall. The campaign organiser was looking for a theme. I suggested a combination of high tea and afternoon tea, and naturally put your name forward. You should be hearing from her soon, Lilly."

Lilly was still smiling when Archie returned with her gin and tonic.

"You look very pleased with yourself. What's happened?"

Lilly told him.

"It looks to me as though you've become an honorary member of the Defoe family, too," he said, giving her a hug. "Look, the first race is about to start."

Lilly settled in to enjoy the rest of the day and was thrilled when Peter and his team won two out of their four races and placed second and third in the others. It was such a relief to have something to celebrate.

If you enjoyed *Storm in a Teacup*, the seventh book in the Tea & Sympathy series, please leave a review on Amazon. It really does help other readers find the books.

ABOUT THE AUTHOR

J. New is the author of *THE YELLOW COTTAGE VINTAGE MYSTERIES*, traditional English whodunits with a twist, set in the 1930's. Known for their clever humour as well as the interesting slant on the traditional murder mystery, they have all achieved Bestseller status on Amazon.

J. New also writes two contemporary cozy crime series:

THE TEA & SYMPATHY series featuring Lilly Tweed, former newspaper Agony Aunt now purveyor of fine teas at The Tea Emporium in the small English market town of Plumpton Mallet. Along with a regular cast of characters, including Earl Grey the shop cat.

THE FINCH & FISCHER series featuring mobile librarian Penny Finch and her rescue dog Fischer. Follow them as they dig up clues and sniff out red herrings in the six villages and hamlets that make up Hampsworthy Downs.

Jacquie was born in West Yorkshire, England. She studied art and design and after qualifying began work as an interior designer, moving onto fine art restoration and animal portraiture before making the decision to pursue her lifelong ambition to write. She now writes full time and lives with her partner of twenty-two years, her dog Oscar and twelve cats, all of whom she rescued.

If you would like to be kept up to date with new releases from J. New, you can sign up to her *Reader's Group* on her website www.jnewwrites.com where you will also receive a link to download the free e-book, *The Yellow Cottage Mystery*, the short-story prequel to The Yellow Cottage Vintage Mystery series.

Printed in Great Britain
by Amazon